*"You are the you that you want to be. Create the world you want to see."*

*~Symone Devereaux~*

# Too Far Ahead

*Getting too far ahead of yourself can get you left behind......*

## Book Two of The Keepsake Box Series

### Chandora Warren

# Table of Contents

# Chapter 1

## ::::My Guy:::::

$W$ell, let me catch you up. It was the year 2000, and it had been two years since I lost Grandma and KEN. It had also been two years since my unfortunate falling out with Mom. Per my normal routine, I woke up at 6:00 on Saturday morning to clean and prepare for my weekend gig. I worked harder than any 20 year old that I knew, but my situation was different than most. I didn't have the familial support that most 20 year olds had. I was in a hole, and I had to claw my way out.

Grandma had assured that I wouldn't ever have to pay rent, but I would have given the house up in a flash if I could have gotten her back instead. I carried so much guilt in reference to not being there when Grandma died. I felt that I had let her down. Technically, I knew that there wasn't anything that I could have done to prevent Grandma's death. Death is inevitable. However, I felt that I had chosen my relationship with KEN over my responsibility to Grandma. That weighed heavily upon me.

If nothing else, I should have kept in contact with Grandma. I should have been around more. Even though I couldn't have prevented her death, there is no way that it should have taken me months to find out that she had passed. I wondered if she thought about me before she died. I certainly thought about her quite a bit.

Everything in that house reminded me of Grandma. Her things still smelled like her. The last dishes that she ate out of were still on the drying mat that was located to the right side of the double sinks—still, after two years. The furniture was the same. I could have made the house more functional, as everything in there was awkwardly positioned. But I couldn't change anything. Somehow, that felt like a betrayal. Grandma hated when someone moved her things, and I couldn't do that to her.

I slept in my childhood bedroom for six months before I finally decided to relocate to the master suite. I found it incredibly difficult to enter Grandma's bedroom, even to turn off her alarm. For six months, I allowed her alarm to ring for ten minutes until it shut itself off. I used it as my personal alarm as well. It was reminiscent of when Grandma used to wake me up for school. Without regards to what I had to do; I woke up at 6:00. While I eventually came around to sleeping in Grandma's bedroom, I still allowed her alarm to wake me up. It was my way of keeping her with me a little. She'd be proud that I wasn't sleeping in all day.

I settled into a free house. And while home ownership had its advantages, it wasn't without its complications. There was no landlord to call when things went awry. It all fell on me, and it was quite expensive. For some reason, it seemed that the house started to fall apart the second I moved in. The roof had a leak, the pipes were rotting, and both porches needed to be replaced. Not to mention the preventative maintenance and taxes. That, too, was on me.

I realized that the house had been in peril for years. As a child, I didn't notice that things were falling apart. Grandma wasn't wonder woman at all. She just made the best out of what she had, and she didn't complain about doing so. I thought about the times when Grandma told me "Londa, everything ain't gonna be perfect. Sometimes, you just gotta make do." But I didn't want to just "make do". I wanted to live comfortably. And a part of me felt that I was paying reparations by fixing the house up the way that Grandma would have if she were able. That was the least I could do, and I was committed to doing it. Grandma was the most consistent catalyst for my guilt, but it wasn't just her. There was so much more to feel guilty about.

It seemed that I was always benefitting from my betrayal. KEN assured that I didn't have to worry about transportation. I thought about him a lot when I sat behind the wheel of that car. I kept the tape that he purchased in the car's cassette player. It was "Where Do Broken Hearts Go?" by Whitney Houston.

I often played that song and reflected on the day that KEN got arrested. I replayed the look on his face over and over again, and it always brought me to tears. Technically, I got KEN arrested. As an additional gut punch, I had received a financial benefit from having done so. None of that was planned, but that fact didn't absolve me of my guilt. I felt solely responsible for KEN's incarceration, even though he'd obviously had the biggest part to play. That's how my mind worked.

I struggled with my feelings about Cassidy as well. I couldn't have taken her with me, as Mom and Ron wouldn't ever have allowed me to do so. I didn't necessarily feel guilty about leaving her, but more so about the possibility that she felt that I'd abandoned her.

Neither Mom nor Ron was particularly attentive towards Cassidy. I'd had several dreams that she was being emotionally and physically neglected. I imagined Mom and Ron banishing her to her bedroom with no affection or human contact. The thought of that was terrifying to me, and it prompted me to create an avenue to be present in Cassidy's life. I didn't have control of much, but that was the one wrong that I felt I was able to right. I was still concerned about her, but I did what I could. That allowed me to sleep a little more easily at night.

But life kept moving right along. And in spite of it all, I was doing fairly well—probably better than what should have been expected. I worked at the gas station during the week and with Sharon on the weekends. Even though I had quit the salon without so much as an advance notice, Sharon allowed me to come back after KEN was arrested. The extra income was needed and most certainly appreciated. I was grateful that she'd found it in her heart to accept me back, in spite of the circumstances.

I was excelling in college as well. Without the distraction of KEN, I was able to concentrate on my studies. Even with the complication of having two jobs, I managed to maintain a 4.2 grade point average. It's obvious that I was always extremely intelligent, but even I was surprised by how easily I was able to get back on track. I was proud of my ability to beat the odds. In spite of it all, I knew that Grandma and KEN would be proud of me.

KEN's absence also allowed me to open myself up to the possibility of dating someone new. Now, that part wouldn't have made Grandma and KEN proud. The situation was problematic—to say the least. And it didn't take long either. I started dating someone new mere months after KEN's arrest. That wasn't planned. But hey, things happen. Though unexpected, I was happy about the addition of my new guy. I loved my new guy.

My new guy encompassed my entire life, but that was the only way that I knew how to function. That was the way I had operated with Ron, Monte, and obviously with KEN. But I was more than happy to allow my new guy to take over. He wasn't like the others. He treated me just the way I wanted to be treated. He did what I needed him to do without having to be asked. Additionally, he helped me out financially. I didn't make a lot of money at either job. Having someone who was willing to fill in the gaps was like hitting the lottery.

Even though Sharon and I reconnected, it wasn't like it was before. I was older, and I no longer viewed her as the knowledgeable older friend who had all the answers. Life had changed me. I felt that I knew what she knew, and I found it difficult to consider the possibility that she knew more about what was best for me than I did.

Additionally, I started to see the cracks in her foundation. Being more exposed to Sharon helped me to understand that her life wasn't all peaches and cream—pun intended. She wasn't as well put together as I thought. If she couldn't manage her own life, why should I allow her to try to manage mine? I didn't find it necessary to bring her into every aspect of my life anymore—and so, I didn't.

I had been dating my guy for two years, and I never really discussed him with Sharon. She always said that I moved too fast, and I preferred not to have that conversation with her—for a variety of reasons. But her claims weren't completely without merit. If you've paid attention to my patterns of behavior, you're probably aware that I'm known to participate in unhealthy relationships—a fact that Sharon was also aware of. The situation with my new guy was certainly no different.

I finished my cleaning and headed to the salon. I always did Cassidy's hair on Saturdays, and I didn't want to be late. Ron was responsible for dropping her off, and he was notoriously prompt. Just in case you're wondering, no! I had not forgiven Ron. I didn't even speak to him. Doing Cassidy's hair was my way of keeping tabs on her without having to deal with Mom or Ron directly. Ron dropped her off and picked her up, without us ever even parting our lips to speak to each other.

Although she was still developmentally behind, Cassidy was able to speak fairly well. I felt relatively comfortable that she would tell me if Ron was attempting to make her the new me. I always asked her leading questions and assessed her behavior. I looked for the signs that everyone missed with me. I had a measure of comfort in the fact that she seemed to have dodged Ron's bullet.

I finally made it to the salon. Sharon and I held idle chitchat, but my mind was a million miles away. I had a date with my guy that night, and I was excited. The day hurried along, and I went home with a good chunk of change in my pockets. It was a good day, indeed.

I showered and got dressed, leaving my hair for last. That wrap was tried and true. In the eight years since Sharon had given me my first wrap, I hadn't deviated much. My hair was beautiful, and it reached the middle of my back. I thought about Toya Boone. I occasionally saw her through some random happenstance, and I was always amused by her appearance. She was fat, and her "good" hair was anything but. It's funny how life works out that way.

I glanced at the clock, proud that I had managed to get dressed on time. I was notorious for being late, and my guy hated that about me. He never argued about it though. He'd say "You're going to be late to your own funeral Little Girl." My response was always the same. "You just make sure you're on time. And if you show up with another woman, I'm going to haunt you both." I loved our playful banter and the way we bounced off of each other. After the dysfunction of KEN, my new guy was like a breath of fresh air.

It was 7:30. He would be there at any moment, and I wanted to look good for him. I gave myself one more detailed look over. I looked good, and I knew it. I knew my new guy would appreciate my effort as well. He was a lover of beautiful things, and he always made sure to let me know that he was impressed. I never had to guess with him. I thought back to the moments when I first encountered my guy. When we first met, nothing in me would have imagined that we would be together. I guess KEN was right to be concerned about him. But that's a different story.

My new guy and I enjoyed a wonderful night. We went to see a popular movie that was out at the time. In the movie, the main character was stranded on a deserted island with no form of human contact. The water reminded me of Ron's spot in the woods, and that irritated me. I hated the water, and I hated that movie. Present day, I still hate that movie. Hurt makes you carry things in ways that you wouldn't ever imagine. After the movie, we went to an amazing restaurant. We ended the night by going to a five star hotel and having five star sex.

My guy wasn't handsome—well, not by my usual standards. But he was good to me, and I was a sucker for that. Dealing with KEN had given me a very narrow perspective of relationships, but my new guy was completely different. He showed me a new side of life—a good side.

The next morning, we ordered room service and had breakfast in bed. We had sex a few times, then it was time for me to go home. If you're wondering, yes. I'd started enjoying sex by that point. My new guy knew exactly what to do. And just as Sharon had told me years prior, sex was much better once I found out what I liked. My new guy showed me what I liked, and there was no going back after he figured it out for me. I remembered the girl who couldn't understand why any woman would voluntarily have sex. Who would have known that I would become a person who felt incomplete without it?

I enjoyed having sex with my new guy, but it was really more about him—just as it had been with KEN. My new guy was an animal. He could easily have had sex three or four times a day. It was a job, but it was my job. I didn't want to consider the alternative. I was aware of what happened when a woman wasn't on her job—I was acutely aware.

We talked on the way home, and I thought about how badly I wanted to take a nap. I was extremely tired. Antonio had worn me out. Yeah, Sharon's Antonio.........

# Chapter 2

## :::: It Wasn't A Choice ::::

$\mathcal{N}$ow, before you give me the side eye, hear me out. It wasn't my intention to sleep with, or be in any way involved with Antonio. I know it sounds cliché, but it "just happened". Really, it did! It all started in 1998. After KEN went to prison, I found a job at a gas station. It didn't pay much, and I was trying to figure things out. Sharon allowed me to come back to work part-time at the salon. But even with the benefit of having two jobs, I was still barely making it.

Grandma had left me the house, but it was old and needed a lot of work. I was solely responsible for those expenses. Additionally, I was in college and responsible for books and tuition. Admittedly, I was a little stressed out.

Things went from bad to worse when the car that KEN had purchased for me broke down. Let me tell you that it was no basic repair. The parts and labor far surpassed what I could technically afford to pay. But it had to be done. I didn't have a choice in the matter.

Sharon offered to make sure that I had transportation to and from work, as my car would be disabled for several days. I was very much aware that it was out of her way. Sharon always arrived at the salon in the morning. Since I worked in the afternoon, I knew she would have to leave work to pick me up. It was a lot, but she was willing to do it. And truthfully, I needed her to do it. I was grateful for her efforts, as I couldn't afford to lose my job. Sharon's generosity took some of the stress out of the situation. So why did I betray her? Like I said, it wasn't planned.

On the first day, Sharon dropped me off at the gas station and headed back to the salon. I didn't stress about the details. I trusted Sharon to arrange for my transportation home, as she said she would. When I reached the end of my shift, I expected to exit the gas station to find Sharon waiting outside for me. But ten minutes before the end of my shift, Antonio came walking through the door—the familiar face. There was nothing special about our initial encounter. We spoke. It was generic and nondescript.

I assumed that Antonio had come inside to retrieve me at Sharon's request. Sharon never liked to get out of her car, and it was certainly past her bedtime. But upon stepping outside, I realized that Sharon was nowhere in sight. Antonio told me that Sharon was tired and had asked him to pick me up instead. Antonio was a night owl, so it made sense that he would still be up at that time. But I didn't care either way. I was exhausted. I was just grateful that someone had arrived to take me home, regardless of who it was.

Antonio and I chatted a little on the way to my house. He asked a lot of questions, and I felt that he was genuinely interested in my responses. He asked about KEN and told me that he had always felt "some kinda way" about him. Unbeknownst to Antonio, KEN had some reservations about him as well. Given the situation, I guess he probably should have. The interaction was comfortable but strange. While I had been around Antonio quite a bit, I realized that I hadn't really had any one on one conversations with him. In fact, I didn't really know him at all.

Antonio dropped me off, and I busied myself with my after work tasks. I ate, studied, and took out my clothes for the next day. I wanted to ensure a smooth run. Sharon was horribly impatient, and I knew better than to make her wait. She was very generous with me, but I knew she would leave me in a heartbeat. I couldn't afford to miss time out of work because I was notoriously late—and I WAS notoriously late. I finished all of my tasks and went to sleep, prepared to do it all again the next day.

Day two started out just as day one had. Sharon dropped me off at the gas station and went back to the salon. But the night didn't end up quite like the one prior. Near the end of my shift, a woman walked into the gas station and asked if I was Shelonda. I told her that I was. I wondered what business she could possibly have had with me, as I hadn't ever seen her prior to that night.

The woman was very pretty. She was tall, slim, and very nicely dressed. Her perfume was expensive, and she wore lots of beautiful jewelry. She was very well put together—on the surface. The woman introduced herself as Cream and told me that Antonio had sent her inside to retrieve me. I walked outside with Cream, where I was greeted by Antonio and another woman who was introduced to me as Peaches. Peaches and Cream. Cute, I thought. In my mind, I believed that they were probably lovers.

Peaches was very pretty as well, but not quite as pretty as Cream. She was shorter and thicker, and also very well dressed. But while she was attractive, it was obvious that Peaches was a little older. Cream joined Peaches in the backseat. Get in, said Antonio. I took my place in the front seat, not realizing that I would permanently earn that spot.

I didn't give much thought in reference to who the women may have been. Antonio always had lots of people around him, as he was a very popular guy. Besides, they could easily have been other friends of Sharon's who also happened to have needed a ride. That wouldn't have been far-fetched. That theory was disproven, however, when we reached the drop off point.

We pulled into an apartment complex in town. Cream exited first. She walked over to Antonio's window and gave him a kiss. It wasn't a sensual kiss. It was a lip peck at most, but it was enough to make me feel uncomfortable about the nature of their relationship. It was obvious that they were more than friends. Although uncomfortable, I said nothing. To be honest, I didn't know what I should say.

After dropping Cream off, Antonio drove around to the other side of the apartment complex. Peaches exited. While she didn't kiss Antonio on the lips, she did kiss him on the cheek. She told Antonio that she loved him. He told her that he loved her as well.

I was shocked! Not only was Antonio involved with those women, but he was audacious enough to be affectionate towards them in my presence. He knew the type of relationship that I had with Sharon, but he obviously hadn't cared enough to hide his indiscretions. I was steamed!

I didn't confront Antonio, but I knew that I would tell Sharon. I owed it to her as a friend. Additionally, Sharon wasn't ever shy about telling me when she felt that something was working outside of my favor. I knew I had to tell her.

The next day, I bombarded Sharon with the news the second I got into her car. I expected her to be angry, maybe even emotional. Sharon and Antonio had been together for a long time. I expected that she would be upset, at the very least. But Sharon wasn't upset. She laughed. She told me that I was a child, and that I had no idea about the complexities of adult relationships. Basically, Sharon told me to mind my business.

I was surprised by Sharon's reaction, and I was irritated by the way she spoke to me. Sharon obviously still perceived me as a child, and that bothered me. That being the case, I decided to allow Sharon to settle her own affairs. She insisted that I mind my business, and I did as I was told.

The days that followed were patterned the same as day two. Sharon picked me up for work and headed back to the salon. Antonio picked me up at night, with Cream and Peaches in tow. I chatted with the women on the rides home. They were nice enough, but I still felt strange about their relationships with Antonio. But since Sharon was so insistent that I mind my business, I saw no need to take issue with the women. They were Sharon's problems.

Friday rolled around, and it was finally time for me to retrieve my car from the mechanic. Antonio picked me up from my house that morning. He took me to pick up my check and to the bank to cash it. Yeah, I know what you're thinking. But back then, paper checks were the norm. Everything required more work in the 90s.

We arrived at the maintenance garage, and the mechanic showed me that the repairs had been completed. We walked inside, and the mechanic walked behind the desk. That'll be $325, he said. $325, I exclaimed. "But you told me that the repairs would cost $250!" The mechanic retrieved my keys from the counter, ensuring that I couldn't run off without paying. The price is the price, he said.

The tears immediately pooled into my eyes. I had a total of $378 to my name. I would be left with $53 out of my check, with two more weeks before I would be receiving another. I knew that I would make money at the salon, but I wasn't ever assured of how much. The hair business was a bit unpredictable, and I didn't have the dedicated clientele that Sharon had. I knew that I would likely have to struggle for the two weeks that were to follow, but what could I do? I didn't have a choice.

I started reaching into my purse to retrieve the money, but Antonio placed his hand on top of mine—a universal request to cease action. He reached into his pocket and handed the mechanic four, crisp one hundred dollar bills. He snatched the keys from the mechanic's hand and motioned for me to follow him outside.

Antonio walked me to my car. He opened the door and gestured for me to sit. I did as he requested. Antonio smiled and addressed me. "People respect you differently when they know you got it." That's what he said to me.

Antonio handed me the keys, and I turned on the ignition. Unexpectedly, the sound of "Where Do Broken Hearts Go?" started blaring through the speakers—the result of me having listened to the tape on the last occasion that I had driven my car. Antonio laughed. Are you really listening to that, he asked. I certainly am, I exclaimed. "This is my favorite song in the whole entire world." Antonio laughed, but complimented me on my taste in music. He said "You have an old soul Little Girl. I like that."  That was the first time that he addressed me as Little Girl.

Antonio pulled out his wallet and passed me a business card. He smiled as he addressed me. "Call me if you need anything…….anything." There was something about the way he repeated the word anything. It was like subliminal messaging—like he needed me to understand that he was accessible to me under any circumstances. Something about that appealed to me.

After giving me his business card and making me understand that it wasn't a rote gesture on his behalf, Antonio handed me $200. Buy yourself something nice, he said. Right that moment, I felt that things were going to go further between us. I was impressed by the way Antonio carried himself. I was also impressed by the way people responded to him. He was so self-assured, and confident. I liked that about him. It wasn't specifically about the money—although the money didn't hurt. It was "THAT" feeling. It was the same feeling that I had when

I saw KEN at my locker for the first time. Something pulled me towards him. It wasn't a choice.

# Chapter 3

## ::::Mixed Signals::::

The next day was a Saturday. I awoke at 6:00 and went to the salon to work with Sharon. Sharon and I went about our usual routines. We chatted, and I did Cassidy's hair. Late in the day, a lady walked in without an appointment. Typically, Sharon would allow me to service the walk-ins. She had an established clientele, and didn't really need the extras. I was usually excited for the opportunity to make a few extra bucks, but that walk-in made me incredibly nervous. Why? Because it was Cream.

Without speaking, Cream bypassed Sharon and walked over to me. You got time for a walk-in, she asked. I smiled stiffly and gestured for her to have a seat. I felt incredibly guilty. I knew that Cream was romantically involved with Antonio. And if I had to be honest, I knew that I was a bit conflicted about my feelings for him as well. For some reason, I felt as if Cream could smell the infatuation on me. That made me uncomfortable.

Cream retrieved a magazine from her purse and showed me a picture of the hairstyle she wanted. I studied the photo, figuring out the best way to execute the hairstyle. Cream smiled, displaying a small diamond in her right canine tooth. She was so flashy, but I loved it. I felt that she carried herself in the way that I would if I were slightly more confident. I could tell that she knew exactly who she was, and she was comfortable in her own skin. I both loved and envied that.

The interaction between Cream and I became more comfortable. We chatted like old friends. Cream was pleasant, but I got the impression that she wasn't very smart—educationally. If I have to be honest, her speech was incomprehensible at times. I found that it was difficult to understand some of the things that she was attempting to say.

I carried on with the conversation nonetheless, hoping to gain some understanding of the situation at hand. I had so many questions. I wondered how she came to be involved with Antonio. I wondered if she knew that Peaches was dealing with him as well. Obviously, that wasn't the time or place to ask. Then again, was there ever an appropriate time to ask those questions?

I completed Cream's hairstyle—impeccably, might I add. She removed an envelope from her purse and passed it over to me. She advised me that she hadn't looked into the envelope, but she was sure that there was enough money to cover her service. That's another reason why I questioned Cream's intelligence. The envelope wasn't sealed. I didn't understand why she hadn't looked inside. I certainly would have.

I opened the envelope to display its contents. Even though I only charged Cream $50 for her hairstyle, Antonio had sent $250. There was also a note, neatly folded in half. That note was like fire in my hands. Sharon was several stations away. But in my mind, she was able to see exactly what was written on that piece of paper. I guess it was that spiritual conviction that Grandma always talked about. That note could easily have said "Have a nice day." But because I was conflicted about my feelings for Antonio, I internalized some guilt over its contents.

I unfolded the note. I don't have to tell you that it didn't say "Have a nice day." The note said "I hope you bought yourself something nice. Let's go out tonight. Call me." My heart was nearly thumping out of my chest. So, it wasn't just me! Antonio felt something too! I stuck the money and the note into the pocket of my smock. I decided to revisit the matter at a more convenient time.

I quietly finished my shift and headed home. I thought about Antonio's note for the entire drive. Without a shadow of a doubt, I was very much aware that I was wrong for even considering Antonio's proposal. Sharon was the only friend that I had, and she had been good to me.

Not only had she taken me in without any responsibility to do so, but she had also provided me with an opportunity to make money. She took an active role in my betterment. Even after I ducked out on her for KEN, she still allowed me to come back to the salon. Sharon inconvenienced herself to ensure that I had a ride to work. She didn't have to do any of those things, but she had done them with no problem—without even having to be asked. Those facts alone should have been enough to make the decision easy. Yet, they weren't.

Just like the situation with Ron and KEN, I saw the benefits of dealing with Antonio. I was young and impressionable when the Ron situation was in play. I was impressed by the fact that Ron bought me jeans and told me that I was pretty. Also being young, I was impressed by the fact that KEN provided a place for me to live and bought me a car.

At 18, with considerably more responsibility, I desired different things. However, my mindset was the exact same. In the week that I had been exposed to Antonio, he had spent $800 on me. That had all happened without me having to do anything or even ask. Something in me wondered what I could get if there was a legitimate effort put forth. I knew that my thought process was flawed, but things weren't easy for me. I would be lying if I said that money wasn't a motivating factor.

I was attending community college, and had every reason to believe that I would be starting at a university shortly thereafter. More advanced education would require more money. I was fortunate to have had the benefit of Grandma's house, so I didn't have the expense of housing. But books and tuition were expensive. I had a little time to save, but I knew that I would still be financially burdened.

Thinking it out, I was already aware that Antonio was dealing with both Peaches and Cream. It was obvious that he was going to cheat on Sharon without regards to my position either way. Why shouldn't I capitalize on his desire to be generous?

But my conscience intervened. I thought about how uncomfortable it would be to see Sharon every day, knowing that I was dealing with Antonio. I thought about how hurt she would be if she found out that I had betrayed her. It was crazy for me to even take Antonio's advances into consideration. Deep down, I knew that there was a difference. Neither Peaches nor Cream had a connection to Sharon. Being Sharon's friend, I knew that knew I owed it to her to be respectful of the relationship that she shared with Antonio—even if he wasn't. I dismissed the thoughts. It was crazy.

I got home and prepared for a night of television and studying. After wrapping my hair and showering, I threw on my favorite sweatpants. I removed my contact lenses and put on my glasses. Looking in the mirror, I wondered why being comfortable was always synonymous with being ugly.

I went into the closet and retrieved my favorite blanket. It was plush and comfortable. But most of all, it was KEN's. I had taken it from his house on the day that he was arrested—along with several other items that belonged to him. Occasionally, I sprayed the blanket with KEN's cologne when it started to wear off. I hadn't washed it since I had taken it from his house. It's crazy, I know. But I missed KEN. The situation was still fresh, and I thought about him a lot.

I pulled out the keepsake box that was given to me by KEN. I looked at our pictures and began to cry. I wondered how a situation with so much promise had gone awry. Things could have been so different. They should have been. The thoughts bombarded my mind.

KEN had turned to drugs and alcohol to cope with his life. Unfortunately for both of us, KEN was a different person when he was under the influence. "Altered" KEN was mean. Altered KEN was ruthless and violent. Altered KEN had raped me when my mind was too immature to even conceive of what was happening.

As far as I was concerned, KEN wasn't really the problem. "My" KEN would have been different if his life had been different, if his parents had been more stable, if he hadn't lost his older brother to violence, if someone had tried to help him instead of just locking him away. If, if, if. Even though my relationship with KEN was unhealthy, I still saw the good in him. I still loved him.

I imagined KEN "fixing" himself in prison and coming home to me. I didn't know how much time he had received, but I figured I would be out of school by the time he was released. He could move in with me and I would help him get himself together. In my mind, that would be perfect. I could be with KEN without the disservice of him having control of my living situation. But that was only plausible if he could forgive me. In my mind, KEN had gone to prison because of me—twice. I didn't know if we could survive that. Deep down, I didn't think that we could.

I put the box away, deciding to watch television and eat ice cream in lieu of studying. Reviewing the contents of the keepsake box had completely taken away my desire to be productive.

Just as I was getting comfortable, there was a knock at the door. Without verification, I immediately knew that it was Sharon. I didn't have much company, and Sharon was the only person who made a habit of coming unannounced. Making matters worse, she had a key. Sharon was notorious for leaving her keys in the car. Somehow, she always deemed it more convenient to knock like the police instead of going back to the car to get her keys.

I left her at the door for a while, hoping that she would get the hint. Since that was not to be the case, I reluctantly decided to answer the door. I flung it open, fully prepared to confront Sharon on her lack of consideration. But upon opening the door, it was I who was met with confrontation. I was surprised to see that it wasn't Sharon, but Antonio at the door.

As a general rule, I find it audacious and intrusive to show up unannounced. I think it shows a basic lack of consideration to arrive without confirmation that your company is desired. That is a concern that should have been expressed to Antonio, as it is important to establish boundaries. But I didn't express my concerns. I simply stepped aside and allowed him to enter.

Once inside, Antonio presented two bags and placed them on my living room table. He explained that my decision to not reach out to him had resulted in the assumption that I would rather stay in, opposed to going out. Again, he was audacious and intrusive, but I allowed him to be so.

Antonio removed the contents of the bags. He passed me a plastic food container and a wrapped cylindrical object that I, unmistakably, knew to be an egg roll. I opened the container. General Tso chicken with extra sauce, lo mein with no onions, and extra broccoli—just like I liked it. I looked up to see Antonio displaying a huge grin. I smiled as well.

Antonio often ordered food for us when I lived with Sharon. And while I was very specific about the way I liked things, he always managed to get it right. I was under the impression that my elaborate hand-written instructions had made that task easier. But with no prompts or instructions, Antonio had managed to remember the minutest of details.

KEN hadn't ever taken the time to do that. I could tell right away that Antonio was observant and attentive. I liked that about him.

Antonio and I had an effortless exchange of entertaining subject matter. He was witty and funny. I knew why Sharon liked him, and I immediately knew that I would be willing to entertain his company on a consistent basis.

In the blink of an eye, it was 11:00. Antonio arose, indicating that it was time for him to leave. He smiled a genuine smile. Something about his smile made me smile. It was warm and inviting. Antonio gave me a hug and left without expressing a desire for anything intimate, not even a kiss. Admittedly, I was confused.

So, maybe I had pegged the situation incorrectly. The fact that Antonio hadn't made any advances caused me to second guess the entire situation. Maybe he was just looking out for me at Sharon's request. Maybe she had arranged a free meal, in the same way that she had arranged for my transportation from work.

Considering those things as options made me feel awful about my lust towards Antonio. Why had I ever considered betraying Sharon? Even more, why would Antonio betray Sharon by dealing with someone so close to her? The whole thing sounded crazy after I thought about it. I decided to dismiss all thoughts of Antonio and get back to the business of living my life. I didn't know where we stood, but I had no desire to deal with Antonio's mixed messages or my mixed feelings.

# Chapter 4

## ::::The Possibilities::::

*T*he week that followed was monotonous and mundane. I went to school, and I went to work at the gas station. I cooked, cleaned, studied, and did homework—all of my usual tasks. And then, it was Saturday.

On Saturday, I awoke at 6:00—just as I did on every other day. I completed my cleaning and headed to the salon. I chatted with Sharon, did Cassidy's hair, and participated in the usual Saturday antics. Near the end of the day, in walks Cream—AGAIN!

Once again, Cream bypassed Sharon without speaking. She walked directly over to me. Before she could ask if I was busy, I smiled and gestured for her to take a seat. The interaction was more comfortable than the week prior, effortless actually. That was probably due, in part, to the fact that I wasn't conflicted about my feelings for Antonio. It made it easier for me to converse without the fear of being found out.

Again, I impeccably styled Cream's hair. And again, she handed me an envelope. Cream hugged me and exited the salon. I opened the envelope, only expecting to find the money that was owed to me. I was convinced that Antonio had been so generous the week before because he identified with my plight. Surely, he wouldn't overpay me to that degree twice. But I was wrong. Just like the week before, the envelope contained $250. And also like the week before, there was a note.

I know it's stupid, but I expected a friendly, lighthearted note—maybe one explaining why he had decided to give me more money. I had settled on the fact that I'd misinterpreted Antonio's intentions the week prior. In my mind, Antonio and I were just friends. That fact was evidenced by his decision not to make a move on me during our previous encounter. I was awful at deciphering the motives of others, and that situation was no different.

I don't have to tell you this, but it wasn't a friendly, lighthearted note. The note took on a more direct and authoritative tone than the one the week prior. "I miss you and I want to see you. Are we staying in or going out?" My heart, again, started beating rapidly. I was known to misinterpret social cues, but I couldn't imagine how that note could have been interpreted in any way other than how I perceived it. Antonio missed me, and he wanted to see me. That was pretty cut and dry. My mind drifted off to the same thoughts as the week before. In a flash, I went from expecting a friendly note to imagining the possibilities. For reasons that many people won't understand, Antonio's attention made me feel special. Why? Let me explain.

The first factor that contributed to my feelings was Antonio's age. Antonio was 30 years old. At 18, I was under the impression that a 30 year old man was "distinguished". Additionally, Sharon perceived me as a child. Receiving attention from a 30 year old man made me feel mature. Antonio had spent time with me, and he seemed to enjoy my company and conversation. Given our age gap, I found that to be an anomaly. He obviously perceived me as a mature adult. He could not have tolerated me otherwise.

The second factor was Antonio's willingness to be inconvenienced. To the best of my knowledge, Antonio had three girlfriends—all of which lived in relatively close proximity to each other. Adding a fourth would certainly present a complication that would make his life less manageable. So why would he unnecessarily present himself with that problem? He obviously didn't need me. For me, the answer was simple. Antonio felt that I was worth it.

Third, was the "pump up". Antonio's attention hugely inflated my self-esteem. Antonio wasn't extremely attractive. Yet, he managed to secure three beautiful women. I didn't think that was by coincidence. Antonio liked pretty things. That point was evidenced by his choices in cars, attire, and women. Having him express an interest made me feel pretty. It made me feel that I could compete with the other women. That was a feeling that I hadn't experienced to that degree.

KEN always told me that I was pretty, but that was different. I appreciated him saying so, but I felt that his claims were more about him making me feel pretty, opposed to his actual belief that I was. I loved him for the gesture, but Antonio's attention made me feel that he REALLY THOUGHT I was pretty. That will sound ridiculous to many. But those lacking in the confidence department will understand.

I put the note in the pocket of my smock, but I didn't disregard the thoughts as I had done the week before. I let the possibilities dance around in my mind. I looked over at Sharon. She was smiling and talking to the client that she was servicing. She looked so happy, and I believed that she was. I had seen Sharon's life. She had a lot to be happy about.

Sharon had a thriving business with a dedicated clientele. She lived in a cute little apartment in town, and drove a cute little car. And even though she knew the truth about Antonio, I was very much aware of why she chose to ignore his indiscretions. Antonio was good to Sharon and anything attached to her. I saw them together, and I knew that they genuinely loved each other. I never doubted that, even after finding out about Peaches and Cream.

The good friend in me saw her happiness and didn't want to be involved in anything that could possibly jeopardize it. But the jealous part of me wanted to be like her. Correction, I wanted to BE her. I had to decide which one of those feelings was the strongest. I don't have to tell you which side I ended up on.

I finished the workday and headed out to my car. I retrieved the note from my smock. I reread it a couple of times, trying to assess how to deliver my response. I didn't want to look disinterested, but I didn't want to look too eager. I reread the note again and began to gather my thoughts. "I miss you and I want to see you. Are we staying in or going out?" I thought of a response and quickly dialed Antonio's number before I could lose my nerve.

He answered the phone on the second ring. Though nervous, I wanted to give the impression that I was confident and self-assured. I gathered myself and delivered my response. "Hey, this is Shelonda. We're going out." Antonio chuckled lightly and told me to be ready at 8:00. It's a date, I said.

I was ready by 7:30—an unusual phenomenon for me. Antonio arrived at 7:50. I'd learn that he was always early. I was excited. I was 18, and I hadn't ever been on a real date. KEN and I didn't date. We spent our days in the woods or ordered food to be eaten inside of the house. The details of the date meant very little. The very act of the date signaled Antonio's willingness to spend time and be seen with me. In my mind, he was taking a huge risk. That had to mean something. Right?

We drove for about an hour before entering a small beach town. It was a cute little area with trinket shops and small cafes. We went to a seafood restaurant. It was one of those fun little places with a large deck and strategically placed imitation crabs. It was a little chilly outside, but I imagined that the restaurant would be packed with tourists in the summer.

Antonio opened the door and gestured for me to enter. I did as he requested. Once inside, he led me to a table near the rear of the restaurant. Antonio pulled out my chair and walked to the other side of the table once I was seated. He smiled, a reassuring gesture that he was happy with how the date was going.

The waitress introduced herself. She attempted to present us with menus, but Antonio stopped her before she was able to do so. He spoke, in his usual confident manner. "We'll have two special deluxe dinners and two glasses of water--one with lemon, one without."

The waitress paused and wrote our order on her sketch pad. Wiiiiiillll there be anything else, she asked. She stretched it out in a way that gave me the impression that she was gathering her thoughts. Antonio looked at her and smiled. But it wasn't his warm, genuine smile. It was dismissive, as if he were encouraging her to leave. He turned his attention to me and presented a genuine smile. Trust me, you're going to love it, he said. The waitress accepted his nonverbal cue and swiftly walked away.

Antonio and I talked and laughed while we waited for our order to arrive. Shortly thereafter, our waitress returned with a cart full of food. It didn't seem that there were enough people in the restaurant to account for the inordinate amount of food on the cart. As she started to unload the food, I understood her initial reaction. All of the food on the cart was ours! There were so many types of seafood, some of which were foreign to me. Four people could easily have eaten off of those meals. There was no wonder why the waitress was confused by Antonio's request for two.

Dig in, he said. I sampled a few of the dishes. I tasted the lobster mac and cheese, garlic shrimp, and Oysters Rockefeller. I was grateful to see Antonio crack open his lobster. I hadn't ever eaten lobster, and I was concerned that I wouldn't open it properly. I imagined myself clumsily biting down onto the shell, as Antonio laughed at my ignorance. I was fortunate to have averted that crisis. I followed Antonio's lead and did as he did.

The conversation followed a natural progression. We laughed and easily moved from one topic to the next. It was easy and comfortable. I never felt awkward or out of place, as I often did. Antonio smiled a lot and touched my hand as he spoke to me. I knew I was in trouble. I experienced the unmistakable feeling of butterflies in my stomach. I hadn't ever experienced that feeling without a desire to dig deeper into the person who had given it to me.

We sat for about an hour before unanimously agreeing that neither of us could possibly ingest another bite. The waitress returned with the check and several "to go" containers. I packed up what I wanted, and we walked up to pay the bill. Antonio gave the waitress $300, and we exited the restaurant. I never actually saw the bill, but I assume that he had tipped the waitress an exorbitant amount. I was impressed by the fact that money was no object for him.

Antonio carried my food with his left hand and interlocked the fingers of his right hand with mine. It was the perfect date. We walked to Antonio's car, laughing and talking the entire time. It was perfect.

# Chapter 5

## ::::Working Women::::

Antonio and I drove for a while before arriving at our next destination. I have to admit that I was surprised by where we ended up. After our amazing date, Antonio had driven us to a strip club—A STRIP CLUB! I hadn't ever been inside of a club of any sort—certainly not one where there was an expectation of nudity. I wondered about his motives. Why had he brought me there?

I nervously looked over to Antonio. He patted my leg and told me that it was ok. I'll make it quick, he said. Make it quick, I thought. I wondered what he was planning to do that would happen quickly. I chuckled when I thought about how my mind worked. Just that quickly, I imagined a strip club set up that was equivalent to fast food service. Opposed to a more credible strip club, the "quick" strip club would offer services that were cheaper and of inferior quality. I imagined some young girl at the strip club drive thru asking if we wanted a side of pole dance with our lap dance. I literally chuckled aloud.

Nonetheless, I accompanied Antonio inside. It was obvious that Antonio was very well-known. All of the men shook his hand, and all of the women gave him hugs. He led me to a door on the other side of the room, never letting go of my hand. There was a sign that read "No Entry". For some reason, I assumed that it would be an office space of some sort. But when Antonio opened the door, I was surprised to see that the room was filled with women—lots of women. They were comfortably walking around, all in various stages of undress. Certainly, they were "too grown."

Before I could question Antonio about the purpose of our visit, a familiar face walked towards me. It was Cream. I hoped my discomfort wasn't readily apparent. She was wearing little more than stilettos and a smile. Cream had a perfect body. She was tall and lean. She had beautiful, perky breasts with nipples that seemed to remain erect with no intervention. Cream grabbed a robe from one of the chairs. I was grateful. Although I was uncomfortable, I could not tear my eyes away from her body. It was amazing.

As I told you before, Cream didn't speak well. I often had to translate her conversations in my mind before responding. It wasn't unusual for Cream to exclude syllables. In some cases, she excluded entire words. I mentally referenced her manner of speaking as a language of its own. She spoke "Cream-nese", a language in which only she was fluent. It was a self-contained inside joke that I only shared with myself.

Cream tied the robe and extended her arms to hug me. "W'chu doone hea Luh Gul". I thought for a second. In Cream-nese, that was the equivalent of someone else asking "What are you doing here Little Girl?" Cream always called me Little Girl, a habit she had indubitably picked up from Antonio.

Antonio told Cream that we were just stopping by. We chatted for a little while before Peaches joined us. Her body was amazing as well. Peaches was short and curvaceous. She was thick, but not at all fat. Her stomach was completely flat and disproportionately tiny in comparison to her hips and butt. Peaches smiled and hugged me as well.

For the first time, I noticed that she had an entire set of gold teeth at the bottom. I looked at Peaches and Cream. I reflected on myself and what I knew about Sharon. It was hard to understand Antonio's type. There were obvious differences between us. I couldn't understand how he could possibly have been drawn to all of us. But I would learn that there was a rhyme and reason to everything that Antonio decided.

Antonio told me that he had to handle some business and that he would be back shortly. He encouraged me to hang out with Cream and Peaches until he returned. I had figured out two things by that point. 1: The establishment was owned by Antonio. 2: Peaches and Cream were strippers.

I chatted with the women for a while before Cream asked if I wanted a drink. I hadn't ever ingested alcohol before. And based on how Ron and KEN acted when they were intoxicated, I wasn't interested. Cream and Peaches dabbled in drugs as well. They, along with a few of the other women, alternated between taking shots of alcohol and snorting lines of cocaine—which Cream offered to me, as well. I imagined that being under the influence made it easier for them to dance on stage. I tried not to judge them, but I remember thinking that they were weak. I couldn't imagine having to be "altered" to deal with my life—and I had been through a lot. Well, I thought I had.

Antonio returned and asked me to follow him to his office. I did as he requested. He asked if I was good with numbers, and I told him that I was. Antonio sat behind his desk and handed me a stack of paperwork— extremely disorganized paperwork. Even as an 18 year old accounting student, it was readily apparent that Antonio's business wasn't doing well. Based on what I witnessed, I was surprised that it hadn't already imploded.

Antonio told me that he had just gotten rid of his "book person" because things didn't seem to be adding up. He was correct in his assessment. Things definitely weren't adding up. I told Antonio that he needed a complete financial overhaul and volunteered my services. Just as I suspected, he was more than grateful to take me up on my offer. I'll be in contact, said Antonio. I smiled, letting him know that I was willing to be contacted—in a personal and professional capacity.

Antonio looked at his watch and said "It's after 12. I'd better be getting you home Little Girl". I laughed and asked him if he liked little girls. He countered my laugh with a laugh of his own. I found that I liked our playful interaction. It was different. It was comfortable.

I stood in front of Antonio's desk and watched as he walked around to me. I turned around to face him, which positioned my back on the front of his desk. Antonio picked me up and placed me on the desk. He positioned his body between my legs and began to kiss me. It was slow and sensual, the type of kiss that KEN and I used to share before he became a bully. Antonio wrapped his arms around my body and hugged me tightly. He smelled amazing.

I took a moment to study Antonio's face as he pulled away. I realized that he wasn't ugly—just not my typical type. Antonio was tall and thick. He wasn't fat, but more of the bulky solid type. He was dark with dark brown eyes. He had thick black hair with deep waves. In that moment, I could see why women were drawn to him. Antonio was confident and assertive. He didn't mind making it known that he was in charge. I liked that.

Antonio lifted me off of his desk, returning me to my original position. He grabbed my hand, and led me out of his office. We said goodbye to the women, and Antonio drove me home. There was never a dull moment with him. Antonio walked me to the door and kissed me in the same manner as he had in his office. He left, with no attempt to come inside. In my mind, it was pretty much a given that I would see him again. It was also a given that things would go further between us. Antonio went on his way, leaving me to wonder when I would see him again.

# Chapter 6

## ::::*I'm Not Going Anywhere*::::

*I* started spending more time at the club after that first night. Initially, it was because I was helping Antonio get his finances in order—which was certainly a task. But after a couple of weeks, I started to enjoy being there. I got to know the dancers, and they were much different from what I expected.

Maybe I watched too much television, but I assumed that they were all in dire straits. In my mind, they were "lost" women who came from broken homes. I assumed that they were all down on their luck and looking for a way to dig themselves out of a hole. Or maybe they were dancing to support their drug habits. I imagined that they left their children alone to fend for themselves while they danced to put food on the table. I learned that reality didn't always meet expectation.

Sure, some of the women were on drugs, but it wasn't at all like I imagined. Dancing wasn't a career of desperation for most of them. Some of them had full-time jobs, but they needed a little extra income. Some of them didn't really need the money, but they enjoyed the job. A couple of them had husbands that came in and enjoyed watching them dance. I was surprised by some of the stories that came out of that room.

I talked to Cream and Peaches and learned quite a bit about them as well. In spite of their perceived closeness, I learned that Peaches and Cream had quite a complicated history. Their relationship wasn't exactly amicable. Through our conversations, I heard varying accounts of how Antonio came to "acquire" the women. I also came to understand the hierarchy and why it was so.

Peaches was the first to enter the situation. She and Antonio met in high school and once enjoyed a monogamous relationship. According to Peaches, Antonio was a "nobody" when they met. She said that he was impressed with the idea of being with someone like her. What do you mean "like you", I asked. Peaches exposed me to a part of Antonio that I hadn't known existed.

By her own admission, Peaches was an orphan who was shuffled around from family to family. By the time she met Antonio, she was a wild 16 year old who knew the streets like the back of her hand. Peaches told me that she met Antonio and was attracted to his quiet confidence. Also 16, Antonio was already a juvenile delinquent in his own right. They connected over their affinity for the street life and need for stability. Peaches was gorgeous back then. Antonio was happy to have snagged the girl that all the other guys wanted.

Both Peaches and Antonio sold drugs on a small scale. But a few years in, it was obvious that Antonio had awful luck with the law. That being said, Peaches felt that they needed a more legitimate business venture. Peaches said that the strip club was her idea. It was her claim that they had both put time and resources into making it work.

Just as things were taking off, Antonio caught a drug charge. As a habitual offender, he was facing serious prison time. Peaches, who didn't have a record at the time, took the charge so Antonio could stay home and build their business. She was sentenced to two years.

According to Peaches, Antonio visited regularly and sent money throughout her entire sentence. She expected that she would come home to a perfect relationship, a grateful boyfriend, and a functioning business. Instead, she came home to Cream and a business that was hanging on by a thread. According to Peaches, she and Antonio weren't ever the same. Antonio had been unfaithful before. That being so,

Peaches assumed that Cream would come and go—just as the others had.

But years later, Cream was still around. It seemed that there was no end in sight. According to Peaches, she accepted that Cream was going to be in the picture, but she made Antonio move out. She decided that she should level the playing field by being able to see other people as well. Peaches admitted to being at the bottom of the relationship hierarchy. But since she was getting what she needed, she decided not to rock the boat. Cream, however, had a totally different account of the events.

The only part of Peaches' and Cream's stories that matched was the fact that Peaches had taken the charge for Antonio. But that's pretty much where the points of agreement ended. According to Cream, she and Antonio were dealing long before Peaches' incarceration. In fact, she was one of the dancers that Peaches brought into the club.

Cream agreed that Peaches and Antonio had met in high school. She also agreed that Peaches was once the "it" girl that all the guys wanted. But she insisted that Antonio wasn't ever faithful to Peaches. She seemed to find it laughable that Peaches would make such a claim.

In Cream's account, Peaches had known all about her. They had even gotten into several physical altercations prior to her incarceration. When Antonio caught his charge, Peaches only agreed to take it because Antonio had "something on her". Cream didn't specify what the "something" was, but I got the impression that whatever it was would have resulted in serious trouble for Peaches if she hadn't done what Antonio asked of her. Cream maintained that Antonio spent most of his time and money on her while Peaches was away. She said that Antonio had only visited Peaches a few times, and only did enough financially to keep her quiet.

After Peaches' release, she and Cream went right back to their bickering. Antonio, who grew tired of it, decided to pull rank. Cream told me that Antonio moved into a place of his own and demanded that she and Peaches accept each other. He moved them into apartments in the same complex, and made them both ride around with him until they could behave like adults.

I laughed at the fact that Antonio had created a childish solution to a very adult problem. Even more amusing was the fact that Peaches and Cream had both obviously agreed to his terms and conditions. Cream told me that they agreed to play nice, and things had eventually calmed down. Even with that being so, they both kept the apartments, and Antonio still chauffeured them around—mainly because they spent a lot of time being under the influence.

Cream swore that she hadn't ever cared about being Antonio's girlfriend, and was basically in it for what she could get. She admitted that she had only fought for Antonio to spite Peaches, who was at the top of the hierarchy at the time. The fact was, whoever was at the top would always get more than everyone else. Cream pushed Peaches down the ladder and enjoyed the perks of being on top. That's why she hadn't felt threatened when Sharon entered the equation a few years later. Everything was working in her favor. She just had to maintain her position.

Now, Sharon's entry was the part that really threw me for a loop. Cream told me that she had introduced Sharon and Antonio. Hmmmmm, that was interesting. Cream never told me how she met Sharon or why she had chosen to introduce her to Antonio. She did say that Sharon had gotten to be "a bit much", which had resulted in them having a falling out.

Hearing Cream's account made a couple of things easier to understand. First, Sharon disregarded the information that I gave her about Antonio's cheating because she already knew about Cream and Peaches. Actually, he was cheating on them with her! Secondly, I understood why Cream walked into the salon and bypassed Sharon. Cream was quite pleasant and usually spoke to everyone she encountered. Her account helped me to understand her behavior. They had a history, and it obviously wasn't pleasant.

I began to see Sharon as less of a victim. She knew exactly who Antonio was, as did Cream. I did, however, feel a little bad for Peaches. Sure, she knew who Antonio was, but she had lost far more than she had gained. Peaches was Antonio's age and had loved him for the entire duration of her adult life. She stuck it out when he was at his worst and took a charge for him. In return, she had to watch him replace her over and over again.

I once asked Peaches why she hadn't just left the whole situation. She only answered that it wasn't that easy. I never asked what that meant. I just understood that there were things that I wouldn't understand. I didn't dedicate a lot of thought to understanding it all. I did, however, put quite a bit of thought into Antonio. Antonio………….

At that time, Antonio and I hadn't gone past the kissing stage. I was just around a lot. Hearing Cream's and Peaches' accounts of their interactions with Antonio should have deterred me from wanting to go further with him. Yet, it didn't. For some reason, I thought that things would be different with me. He treated me differently than he treated them. I saw the benefits of dealing with Antonio, and I overlooked every sign that I should have seen. Story of my life.

Things changed between me and Antonio a few weeks after our first date. Antonio asked me to come to the club to assist him with some paperwork. He unlocked the door to his office and left me alone to do my business. That was our usual routine. Initially, things went as they had on every other occasion, and I had no expectation that the encounter would be any different. Boy was I wrong!

Approximately an hour into my visit, Antonio entered the office and locked the door behind him. That was unusual. Typically, Antonio would leave the door unlocked because he didn't like to arise once he was seated. If anyone knocked, he usually instructed them to enter through the unlocked door. While doing the paperwork, I usually sat behind his desk to make things easier. If Antonio ever entered, it was customary for him to sit in the chair that was placed on the other side.

I stood as Antonio walked towards me, assuming that he wanted to claim his place behind his desk. Unbeknownst to me, he had other plans. Antonio placed his arms around my waist and kissed me as I stood. He and I had kissed a few times, so I wasn't expecting things to go any further. But when Antonio started to kiss my neck, I knew the experience would be different.

To this day, the details are still very vivid in my mind. I tend to hold on to things that way. I was wearing a denim dress with buttons down the entire front. Antonio released each button one by one as he kissed me. It wasn't clumsy like when KEN tried to unfasten my bra. It was smooth and effortless. I could tell that Antonio knew what he was doing. He was experienced.

I wasn't wearing a bra that day, which worked out perfectly for the occasion. Antonio started at my neck and worked his way down. Initially, I felt a little insecure. I'd seen the bodies of the women that Antonio was used to, and mine couldn't compete or compare. I was slim like Cream, but short like Peaches. Unfortunately, I didn't have either of their "assets".

Thinking about it now, my body was perfectly acceptable for that of an 18 year old. My breasts were a small A cup, and my butt was of an average size. Even so, they were both perfectly proportioned for my age and stature. I had been in many adult situations, but I was technically a child just one year earlier. My body was just fine, but my insecurities made me second guess everything about myself.

I wasn't insecure with KEN—well, not to that degree. I guess I knew that KEN would have limited expectations. My body was typical for a girl in our age range. But Antonio was different. He was a grown man. I immediately began to experience a bit of anxiety. What if my performance wasn't up to par? What if the sex wasn't mature enough for him? All of those thoughts crossed my mind in the time it took for Antonio to move from my neck to my shoulder.

My heart began to race, and I was noticeably shaking. Antonio smiled at me, displaying his perfectly straight white teeth. They were beautiful. In that moment, he was beautiful. Antonio traced my lips with his finger. I was incredibly aroused. He made me feel that he desired me. He made me feel wanted.

Just relax, said Antonio. He instructed me to sit down in the chair. I did as he requested. Antonio got onto his knees and started kissing my breasts. He caressed my back while doing so. Antonio traced my nipples with his tongue, causing them to become erect. My body reacted to his touch in a way that I hadn't ever experienced prior to that point. I had certainly been aroused by KEN, even by Ron. But the experience with Antonio was different. It was as if he knew exactly what I wanted, needed, and desired.

After leaving my breasts, Antonio worked his tongue down to my stomach. It was very sensual, and my body responded appropriately. I thought he would stop there, but he didn't. Antonio continued to work his way down, exploring parts that hadn't ever been touched by a tongue. Keep in mind that I was 18. Present day, oral sex is almost a given. But at 18, most of the guys that were in my age range treated oral sex like a germ. It was nasty. But Antonio seemed to enjoy it.

Antonio started by gently kissing the exterior, while caressing the outsides of my legs. He licked in a gentle up and down motion. I tried to control the moaning, a task that was becoming increasingly difficult with every second that passed. Antonio pushed my legs up, causing my knees to come to rest on my breasts. While initially soft and sensual, Antonio began to eat with a ravenous ferocity. He fully inserted his tongue and began a rapid sequence of in and out motions.  All attempts to control the moaning had become futile at that point. I locked my legs around his head and grabbed the sides of the chair. And there it was, my first official orgasm.

The "Accidental O" was a notable point in time that has always stuck with me, but the situation with Antonio was different. It was no accident. Antonio was very skilled in that department, and he knew it. He looked up at me as I reached my climax. He smiled and came up to kiss me. The thought of that would normally have been enough to disgust me, but I was intrigued. I was incredibly turned on. Antonio smiled at me. He got back onto his knees and started all over. And just like that, one orgasm became two.

Antonio asked me to stand. I did as he asked. He kissed me as he buttoned my dress. He jokingly advised that we had done enough work for the night. We both laughed. Antonio didn't attempt to have sex with me, and I loved that. There was something incredibly sexy about the idea of a man who wanted to please me without having the expectation of getting anything in return.

That was the night that most of my consideration for the other trio of women went out of the window. Their roles in the equation became far less important. It was official. I was there, and I wasn't going anywhere.

# Chapter 7

## ::::*Clownfish And Anemone*::::

*T*hings moved quickly from that point. I became a regular fixture at the club—sometimes for work, sometimes for play. I loved being there. Antonio paraded me around like I was a princess. I loved that too.

As I started to spend more time around Antonio, I began to realize something. It was obvious that he viewed me differently than he viewed Cream and Peaches. He didn't seem to care what they did. He didn't care that they flirted with and entertained other men at the club. Antonio and I didn't have a formal relationship arrangement, but he made it obvious that I was off limits to anyone who frequented the club. Out of respect for him, no one even made the attempt.

I began to understand that Antonio had a value system. He treated everyone and everything according to where they fell. I loved feeling that Antonio valued me enough hold me in a certain regard. He didn't want anyone else to have my attention, and he didn't want me to be tainted by the life that he lived. I remember the exact moment when that became apparent to me.

One night I came to the club to spend time with Antonio. It was a social visit, so I wasn't camping out in the office. Antonio was in his office, and I was in the dressing room with the girls—not at all an unusual phenomenon. Cream addressed me, in her usual diction. "You look tied Luh Gul." I translated her statement in my mind. "You look tired Little Girl." I explained to Cream that I was exhausted. Between work at the gas station, school, the salon, and Antonio, I was certainly spreading myself too thin.

Cream pondered for a moment before addressing me again. "Hy ole ar ya Luh Gul?"=How old are you Little Girl? I told her that I was 18. Cream responded with a question. "Hy badja wonna be grown?"=How bad do you want to be grown? I was confused by her question, but Cream and I had built a rapport based on the fact that we were both quite witty. I advised her that I hadn't come to the club to audition for adulthood. She laughed, and I laughed as well.

Cream, again, addressed me. "Wont sumn ta keepya up?"=Want something to keep you up? Before I could respond, Cream reached into her purse and pulled out a sandwich bag with white powder inside. Being aware of Cream's habits, I was pretty sure that the bag contained cocaine. She attempted to pass the bag over to me. You know I don't do that, I said.

Just as Cream was retracting her arm, Antonio walked into the dressing room. I watched his eyes zone in on Cream and enlarge. Antonio marched over to Cream and knocked the bag out of her hand. He then proceeded to throw her against the wall and put his hands around her throat. I watched the faces of the other women. Though everyone looked uncomfortable, no one spoke. You could have heard a pin drop.

What is wrong with you, Antonio screamed. Cream looked terrified. I couldn't blame her. I was terrified, and I wasn't even the victim of his rage. Antonio threw Cream onto the floor. I watched her sob in between her gasps for air.

Antonio grabbed my arm and pulled me out of the dressing room. He dragged me all the way through the club to his office. Onlookers stared curiously as he pulled me inside and slammed the door. I was immediately taken back to the night that KEN raped me in my bathroom. I was terrified and shaking like an abused animal.

Antonio screamed loudly as he shook me by my arms. "Don't you ever let me catch you doing that stuff!" His voice was loud and commanding. It seemed to reverberate through the walls. I didn't do it, I screamed. "I didn't even have the intention to do it!" Antonio released my arms. Neither of us spoke for a moment. Unexpectedly, I started to sob. I didn't even feel it coming on. I'm so sorry, said Antonio. He hugged me so tightly that it was physically uncomfortable. Antonio released me from his embrace. Although they never fell, I could see that he had tears in his eyes.

Antonio exercised an extreme amount of strength in fighting back the tears. He bypassed me and locked the door. The sound of the lock bolting terrified me, causing me to sob even harder. Antonio asked me to have a seat. I did as he requested. Please stop crying, he said. I sat for a moment, attempting to regain my composure. After I had collected myself enough to listen, Antonio addressed me. He did so in a way that only he could.

Now, there's something that you have to understand. Antonio watched the nature channel more than anyone else that I knew. His viewing practices often became points of comparison in his analogies. That day was the first of many times in which Antonio would use his extreme knowledge of animals to make a point to me. It wouldn't be that last, but it was certainly the one that has stood out throughout the years. The conversation went a little something like this:

"Baby, let's talk about something. What I'm about to tell you is serious, and you can't take it lightly. I know you've probably heard stories and speculation, but let me give it to you from the horse's mouth. You know that I have been dealing with these women for years, and it's obvious that I care about them to some degree. That being the case, you must be wondering why there's so much variation between the way I treat you and Sharon and the way I treat Cream and Peaches. The answer is simple. It all boils down to respect. Cream and Peaches are like a troupe of shrimp. They're scavengers that run in packs. Wild shrimp eat plant debris, worms, dead fish, clams, crabs, snails, and whatever other decaying matter that they can find. Cream and Peaches are means to an end people. They do what it takes to satisfy whatever need they have at the time, whether it's money, drugs, attention, or anything else. Those types of people can't be trusted. Thus, they can't be respected. You're different Londa. We're different together. You're like a clownfish, and I'm like a sea anemone. Clownfish are beautiful and delicate creatures. They're typically found residing in close proximity to sea anemones. Though typically predatory, the anemone develops a mutually beneficial relationship with the clownfish. Anemones are armed with stinging cells that release toxins when touched by prey or predators. The clownfish, however, develops a layer of mucus that makes it immune to the anemone's deadly toxins. That makes it possible for the clownfish to exist in a space that most other species could not. The anemone's toxins protect the clownfish, as they would be easy prey otherwise. They also provide food for the clownfish. In return, the clownfish protects the anemone by chasing away certain species of predatory fish. You see, one hand washes the other. But here's the thing. Anemones anchor themselves to the sea floor. If the clownfish strays too far away, the anemone can't protect it. I'm trying to be a sea anemone for you. If you start moving as the shrimp do, I can't trust you.  If I can't trust you, I can't respect you. And if you're too far away from me, I can't protect you. Cream and Peaches are predators. They will chew you up and spit you out before you've ever even realized that you were in their mouths. That's why I was so angry earlier. I don't want you to get swallowed up Little Girl. You understand that right?"

I understood where Antonio was coming from, and I appreciated his perspective. Additionally, I'm a bit of a sapiosexual.  I was impressed by Antonio's ability to convey his position in such an intellectual manner. His extensive knowledge of animals was appealing to me, and his analogies always made perfect sense. I knew that Antonio saw me differently than he saw Cream and Peaches, and his explanation made me feel special. That probably would have been the end of the encounter, but Antonio decided to add a layer of complexity to his analogy.

I stood and draped my arms around Antonio's neck. I gave him a peck on the lips and told him that I understood his point. You don't have to worry about that, I said. "I have no desire to do drugs, and certainly wouldn't at Cream's request. I appreciate you trying to protect me though. That's cute." I turned, expecting to be on my way, but Antonio stopped me. Wait, he said.

"There's one other thing. In addition to being beautiful and delicate, clownfish are fiercely loyal and monogamous. They typically live in pairs and devote themselves to their partners. Can you do that for me? Only me?"

While I had initially been willing to accept Antonio's point of view, he had certainly thrown me for a loop. Sure, he had some valid points as they related to Cream and Peaches. But Antonio's request for one-sided monogamy was a different matter entirely. It created a desire to counter with an analogy of my own. I laughed a little before speaking. It became my intent to have Antonio remise. I addressed him.

"So, I was going to allow you to present your analogy unchallenged, but you seem to have excluded some important factors. Yes, the sea anemone protects and feeds the clownfish. But it isn't a deliberate action on its behalf. It is the simple nature of the sea anemone, and it is done with very little effort. The clownfish has to develop the mucus covering that makes it immune to the anemone. If it were ever washed away, the anemone would become predatory towards the clownfish as well. The anemone isn't just some generous creature. It also receives a benefit from providing the meals. The clownfish helps to preen the anemone by eating algae and other food leftovers. Without the deliberate action of the clownfish, the leftover debris would be of serious detriment to the anemone. Additionally, the anemone anchors itself to the sea floor. By default, it is never expected to make a move. It will remain comfortable in that space with everything it needs. And now, you want me to be a clownfish, loyal and monogamous. Meanwhile, you will be an anemone. You will collect clownfish at your leisure and kill them when the mucus washes away. By your logic, it doesn't seem that one hand washes the other at all. It seems that one hand extends itself and allows the other hand to pump the soap. By virtue of being what it is naturally designed to be, one hand exerts no effort in providing friction to the other hand. By default, the one hand receives the benefit of being clean, by simply existing. Let's call a spade a spade Antonio. You provide and protect because that's what you do. By your own admission, Cream and Peaches are shrimp. Yet, you still do for them what you do for me. But we all serve a purpose for you as well. I surmise that I am still here because I'm good with numbers and I know how to move things around. While saying that you are shooting out toxins to protect me, don't forget that I'm eating the algae. I am as beneficial to you as you are to me. If Cream or Peaches could cook the books, I wouldn't even exist."

Antonio looked legitimately hurt and confused. I felt bad for saying the words after they left my mouth, but it was too late to take them back. Is that what you think, he asked. Before I could answer, Antonio picked me up and sat me on his desk. He positioned his body between my legs. Antonio kissed me slowly and deliberately. He looked into my eyes and addressed me.

"I've taken in everything that you've said, and you're right. You are an asset to me, as are Peaches and Cream. But you're certainly wrong otherwise. You're around because I want you here. Ask yourself if I spend this amount of time with anyone else—even Sharon. That has to mean something to you. Doesn't it? I know that this situation isn't fair to you, but it's how we live. I'm not going to promise you anything that I won't follow through with, including monogamy. It may seem selfish to ask you to dedicate yourself to me, but I can't imagine you being with anyone else. I'll do almost anything to prevent that from happening. I love you Little Girl, and not in the way that I love Cream and Peaches. I am in love with you. I'm sorry that I've failed to make that obvious to you. But now that I know how you feel, I will make it right. I'll do what it takes to make sure you know where you stand with me. Will you open yourself up to the possibility of allowing me to do that?"

That was the first time Antonio told me that he loved me. I shook my head, indicating that I would allow him to show me where I stood. Maybe Antonio didn't know it, but I only wanted to be with him. Entertaining someone else would have felt like as much of a betrayal to myself as it would have been to him. That's how much I cared about him. Antonio kissed me while caressing my back. I want you, he said. "Let's go to your place." I snickered. I guess we've now upgraded from office sex, I said. Antonio didn't laugh. We can't do this here, he said.

The ride to my house was extremely sexually intense. It started with a simple kiss at the stop light. After taking off, Antonio started to unbutton my jeans with his right hand. He reached into my pants and slid my underwear to the side. I closed my eyes and reclined my head. Antonio smiled as he inserted his fingers in and out, only stopping periodically to taste them. Just as I was about to reach my climax, he stopped. I opened my eyes to find that we were parked outside of my house. Antonio smiled. Let's go, he said.

The moment we were inside, Antonio picked me up and took me into my bedroom. It was the most passionate sexual exchange that we had ever experienced. Antonio slowly stroked in and out. He whispered in my ear, only pausing to allow me to respond. He asked the questions, and I answered them.

"Antonio: You love me Little Girl?

Me: You know I do.

Antonio: Tell me.

Me: I love you Baby.

Antonio: You want me?

Me: You know I do.

Antonio: Tell me.

Me: I want you, more than anything.

Antonio: I want you to be mine. Will you be mine? Only mine?

Me: YES!

Antonio: Tell me!

Me: I'M YOURS! I'M ALL YOURS!

Antonio: That's my Baby."

And with that, we simultaneously experienced the most extreme orgasms. It was amazing. Antonio didn't have to worry about sharing me with anyone else, and he knew it.

After we were done, Antonio stood and got dressed. He told me that he had to go back to the club to get Cream and Peaches. You riding, he asked. I told him that I was exhausted and needed to go to sleep. Antonio told me that he would be back after dropping them off. I reached into my nightstand and gave him an extra key. Let yourself in, I said. Antonio kissed me and left to complete his task.

Shortly thereafter, Antonio returned. He slid into bed behind me and held me close. He whispered in my ear. "I love you Little Girl." I reciprocated his statement. I fell asleep in his arms, feeling loved and protected by my anemone.

# Chapter 8

## ::::*Taking Over*::::

*I* fell in love with Antoni❖—madly in love. In my young mind, he was everything that I ever wanted, and so much more. I was satisfied with what Antoni❖ presented to me because I wasn't even aware that I should expect more. I remained comfortable in the situation for about a year before I felt the itch of change.

There was already a shift in the hierarchy. Peaches comfortably maintained her position at the bottom, but I had basically taken over as the new Cream. Cream didn't seem to care though. She went on about her normal business, as if nothing had changed. Neither of the women ever acted any differently towards me.

I was happy to knock Cream and Peaches down a couple of notches, but it wasn't ever my intention to take Sharon's place—well not initially. In spite of the fact that I was sleeping with Antoni❖, I loved and respected Sharon too much to try to "take" him. I was simply putting in my bid and reaping the benefits of being one of his girls. In my mind, I wasn't doing anything more to Sharon than what she had done to Cream.

But after a while, I began to notice the disparity between us. Admittedly, I got jealous. I realized that Antoni❖ was willing to invest in THINGS for me, but he was willing to invest IN Sharon. Antoni❖ filled my gas tank, but he bought Sharon a car. He paid bills at my house, but he paid Sharon's mortgage. He got my breasts done, but he bought a salon for Sharon. Those points weren't ever lost upon me, but I was patiently waiting my turn.

I was taking it all in stride until Antoni❣ took Sharon to Jamaica for a week. That changed everything for me. I was initially happy being taken to five star hotels, but I felt slighted when I realized that Antoni❣ was going out of his way to create experiences with Sharon. He wasn't doing that with me. That was the straw that broke the camel's back.

I took over Sharon's clients while she was in Jamaica with Antoni❣. As the days went on, I started to resent her more and more. She was off creating memories with "my man" while I was keeping her business afloat. Adding insult to injury, I had to listen to everything that was being said around me.

Women would come into the salon and brag on how well Antoni❣ treated Sharon. I got so tired of hearing it! "Antoni❣ is so good to Sharon." "I need an Antoni❣ in my life." "Blah, blah, blah." A few of them even suggested that I should aspire to be like Sharon to ensure that I could get a guy like Antoni❣. I was livid! GET a guy like Antoni❣? I HAD a guy like Antoni❣---ANTONI❣! I knew then, that Sharon had to go. Well, she didn't have to GO, but she certainly had to go down in the hierarchy. I spent the entire week fuming and thinking about how I was going to "out woman" Sharon. My soul wouldn't have rested otherwise.

I put a plan into motion. I started "racing" Sharon when she and Antoni❣ returned from Jamaica. I tend to liken our competition to an actual race. Sharon and I were competing, and Antoni❣ was both the coach and the prize. The odds were in my favor from the very beginning. How so? Let me explain.

The first factor that worked in my favor was age. I was 19 and Sharon was 26. I was younger and fresher. I had more energy and endurance, both of which are advantages in any race. Sharon obviously had a hold on Antoni❣, but one thing couldn't be disputed. She was older, and Antoni❣ liked younger women. No amount of effort on her behalf could make her younger.

The second factor was the fact that I was being spoon-fed the formula for success by the coach. Antonio shared all of Sharon's weaknesses with me, allowing me to avoid making the same mistakes. If she didn't cook, I cooked all the time. Antonio told me that Sharon was always too tired for sex. Consequently, I was never too tired for sex— even when I was. There was no chicanery involved. I simply did what she didn't and capitalized on where she fell short. It was a formula that was as old as time. It was the equivalent of starting a race with the understanding that your competitor has an injured knee. It allows you to strategize in a way that almost certainly ensures victory. That's what Antonio did for me.

The third factor was advanced knowledge. Truthfully, Sharon wasn't even aware that she was involved in a race. That was unfortunate for her. Sharon leisurely strolled through her relationship with Antonio, comfortable and unassuming. She never attempted to walk any faster. She wasn't in a rush. I sprinted past Sharon on a regular basis. Her only critique was the fact that I was moving too fast, never knowing that she was actually losing the race. It's so easy to win when the other party isn't even aware that they're competing. Like I said before, it was designed for me to win.

I put the plan in motion as soon as Sharon and Antonio returned from Jamaica. I welcomed him back with open arms. I told him that I missed him, and I went above and beyond the call of duty.

I didn't wait for him to tell me that Sharon was too tired to cook. I invited him over for dinner before she even thought about it. I didn't just cook, but I cooked whatever he wanted, whenever he wanted it. Antonio would sometimes arrive in the middle of the night and request a meal. Without regards to how tired I was, Antonio always got what he requested. No questions asked.

I never let Antonio go to sleep without the understanding that my body was accessible to him. I worked like a horse. Between the gas station, the salon, school, and Antonio, I was exhausted more often than not. But it was a no brainer for me. I would be there to supply whatever he wanted and needed, at whatever cost. I worked overtime to be anything and everything that he needed. Sharon couldn't compete. It was nearly impossible for her to be able to. It wasn't long before I phased her out—just as she had done to Cream.

I recall the exact day that I realized that I had taken Sharon's place. It was early on a Saturday morning, and I was preparing to go to work at the salon. I was finishing my breakfast when Antonio came bouncing through the door. I was surprised to see him. Antonio had a key and was welcomed to come and go at his leisure, but it wasn't his normal tendency to even be awake that early.

Antonio walked over to the table and kissed me. He had news. I could tell. What brings you here this early, I asked. He told me that he had a surprise for me, and he didn't want to wait for me to get off of work. I wasn't surprised that Antonio had a surprise. He always had a surprise for me. I would often come home to money or jewelry without ever having seen Antonio. So what is it, I asked. Antonio smiled. You're gonna love it, he said. And I knew that I would.

That was the thing about Antonio. He was extraordinarily observant. I never had to tell him anything. He picked up on the things that I liked, and presented them to me in the most unexpected and loving ways. My wants and needs weren't ever lost upon him—even when he didn't understand them. Antonio always told me that I was strange. However, he never stopped indulging in my strangeness. I loved that about him.

Antonio laughed at my musical selection, but he allowed me to sing my favorite songs at the top of my lungs—uninhibited and unjudged.

He watched me sing, laughing and shaking his head. He never stopped me.

Antonio found it strange that I never moved Grandma's dishes off of the drying mat. Yet, he never moved them either. He simply purchased a drying rack that took residence in the second sink. That became our official place for wet dishes, and we never discussed it.

Antonio often talked about how I liked my grits with sugar, opposed to butter and pepper. But in ordering food for me, he was always sure to order my grits with sugar. My eggs were always scrambled with lots of cheese. My bacon was always just a little too soft for his liking. Yet, he ordered my food that way every single time.

Antonio always made sure to present things to my specifications. I was always made aware that he cared enough to put emphasis on the details. He always made sure that I had things the exact way that I wanted them, even when my preferences were in opposition to his.

Antonio loved braids, and he wanted me to wear them all the time. And even though I usually went against everything that he chose for me, he never had a problem paying. He always swore that he wouldn't, but I knew he would. Antonio paid for everything.

But it wasn't just about the money. Sure, Antonio spent money on me, but he spent time as well. Our relationship reminded me of the relationship between him and Sharon. Antonio brought food over for me, and also for Cassidy when she was with me—just as he did when I lived with Sharon. He remembered her favorite foods and did crazy things to make her laugh. I loved that about him. I loved the way that he loved me. I loved the fact that he loved anything that was connected to me. That's who Antonio was.

But back to the surprise. Antonio took my hand and led me outside. I was astonished by what I saw. Antonio had purchased a car for me! But it wasn't just A car. It was THE car! My dream car! It was a 1999 Jaguar--black with tan interior. It was the epitome of luxury at that time. I often joked that I would purchase that car if I ever won the lottery, but Antoni❖ had purchased it for me. It was mine, free and clear. I didn't even have to hit the lottery. I was ecstatic! Antoni❖ named the Jaguar Lady. He said she was beautiful, luxurious, and powerful—just like the perfect lady.

And Lady was absolutely perfect. Not only that, but she signaled a shift in the hierarchy. Yes, Antoni❖ had purchased a car for Sharon, but he didn't purchase THAT car for Sharon. He bought her a cute little domestic sedan that was good on gas, but it wasn't luxurious. MY car was luxurious! That was the thing about Antoni❖. You always knew where you were in the value system, based on what he was willing to do for you. He was willing to do a lot for me, and that let me know where I stood.

I jumped on Antoni❖, wrapping my legs around his waist. She's absolutely beautiful, I screamed. Let's stay home today, said Antoni❖. I contemplated his request for a moment, but I had already promised Cassidy that I would do her hair at the salon. Of all the areas in which I had fallen short, the one thing that I tried to maintain was my relationship with Cassidy. I didn't want to disappoint her.

I told Antoni❖ that I HAD to go to work, but I would thank him properly when I returned home. He passed me the keys to the car, and told me that he'd wash my dishes so I could go on to work. Hurry up and get there so you can hurry up and get back, he said. Antoni❖ told me that he would be there waiting for me upon my return. I grabbed my things from the house and kissed him goodbye. I sat behind the wheel of my brand new car, overwhelmed with happiness and excitement.

I turned on the ignition. To my surprise, "Where Do Broken Hearts Go?" was playing softly through the speakers. I looked at Antoni❖. He was smiling ear to ear. I smiled as well. Not only had he purchased the car of my dreams, but he had also purchased the Whitney Houston CD and inserted it for that very moment.

You have to understand my way of thinking. Money was nothing to Antonie. He spent money all day. But I fell in love with the way he loved me. His smile informed me that he was happy to have made me happy. I can't even describe the love that I felt for him in that moment, and I didn't think that he could possibly do anything to top that feeling. But, he did. He always did.

I was thinking, said Antonie. "What do you think about going to Hawaii?" And THAT'S when I knew that Sharon was number two.

# Chapter 9

## :::: Unmet Obligations—Part 1 ::::

After I took Sharon's place, I was everywhere with Antoni❖. Inevitably, I arrived at a point where I started to neglect my obligations. I was often late going to work at the gas station. Sometimes, I failed to make it in altogether. I wasn't concerned about the money, as I didn't really need it. Antoni❖ paid me to work his books, even when I didn't work. I worked at the gas station when I wanted to, and that honestly wasn't very often.

Antoni❖ consumed most of my time, so much so that I failed to meet the submission deadline to start college at the university. I finished my second year of community college with a 4.2 grade point average and unlimited options for college transfers. Yet, I spent my time keeping up with Antoni❖ and making sure that I remained at the top of the hierarchy. I certainly never neglected that obligation.

The plan was to take a semester off to get everything together. That way, I'd be all set to start in the winter. I don't have to tell you that it didn't happen that way. Life moved fast and college moved much too slowly. Being honest, my education wasn't on the agenda at that moment. I used the missed deadline as an excuse. Truthfully, I was just busy living the life. I loved the life and all the perks that came with it.

After a while, Sharon told me that she no longer needed me at the salon. She said that business had slowed down, but I knew it was deeper than that. Sharon had another assistant who stayed on after I left. I couldn't be upset with her though. Sharon never knew if I was going to be available. And when I did show up, I usually came in late or left early—

depending on what Antoni☕ had going on. She couldn't depend on me. She and I were both aware of that fact.

I was bothered that I had let Sharon down—again. I know that sounds ridiculous. I was able to look her right in her face, while knowingly sharing a boyfriend with her. But that was different. Sharon wasn't aware of my relationship with Antoni☕. No harm, no foul. She couldn't be hurt by information to which she hadn't been exposed. But my negligence towards the job was another situation entirely. Time and time again, Sharon had been there for me and allowed me to work at the salon. At several points in time, working there was the only thing that helped me to get by. But in every single situation, I had let her down for the benefit of my relationships. I honestly did suffer some guilt over that.

But that was the end of my sadness over the situation. Being let go from the salon was actually a relief. I didn't really need the money anymore, and it was a bit of a chore. I was only there because I thought Sharon needed me. Getting fired allowed me the opportunity to direct my attention where I most desired—spending time with Antoni☕. And trust me when I tell you that I took full advantage.

The only other drawback to leaving the salon was the fact that I wouldn't be there to do Cassidy's hair on Saturday's. Cassidy loved coming to the salon and pumping the chairs up and down. But there was an easy solution. It wasn't unusual for me to keep Cassidy at my house from time to time. I had everything that was needed, so I decided that I could just as easily fulfill my obligation to her at home. There were no fancy chairs, but Cassidy would still be able to get her hair done. Additionally, I would still be able to keep tabs on her. That was enough for me. But because things were about to change, I had to reach out to Mom and Ron, a task that I absolutely hated to complete. But……I had to.

I dialed the phone number to Mom and Ron's house. My only intent was to have Ron deliver Cassidy to my house, opposed to the salon. Surprisingly, it wasn't Ron who answered the phone, but Mom. I hadn't talked to Mom since I attempted to get my portion of Grandma's insurance money. By that point in time, everyone had caller ID. That feature ensured that Mom wouldn't ever answer the phone when I called. And up to that point, she never had. I was perfectly ok with that, but I wondered why she had decided to break the code on that day.

Mom only issued a salutation, but there was something very strange in her tone. It was laced with sadness. "Hello?" I paused when I heard her voice, but decided that I would follow through with the intent of the call. I addressed her, as if we hadn't been estranged for years. "Hi Mom. I need Ron to bring Cassidy to the house tomorrow instead of bringing her to the salon." Mom paused, but I could hear the break in her voice. "Londa, I have to tell you something." I didn't know what I was about to hear, but I immediately knew that it would be devastating. I had the same feeling that I had when I found out that Mom had tried to commit suicide. My eyes began to water, fully anticipating bad news.

Ron's in prison, said Mom. I sat quietly for a moment, as I didn't know what was expected of me. I couldn't imagine that Mom expected me to be saddened by Ron's predicament. I assumed that she just wanted me to understand that Ron was in no position to deliver Cassidy to me. Or maybe, she needed assistance in providing some sort of resources for him. Neither scenario was of any consequence to me. Mom would just be responsible for bringing Cassidy, and Ron would rot in prison. They were no brainers for me. But just as I was about to ask if she was willing to bring Cassidy over, Mom broke into tears. Before I could inquire about the source of her sadness, Mom blurted out something that I hadn't ever expected to hear. "I'm sorry Londa. I am so sorry."

I was shocked and confused. Mom hadn't ever apologized for anything, and we definitely had a past that should have prompted her to do so. Even after everything that had occurred between us, a small part of my heart softened. I addressed her. "Mom, are you ok?" The words that Mom uttered took me by surprise and took me back to a very dark place in my life—a place that I had struggled to forget. Mom exhaled. She then, addressed me.

"Londa, I want to apologize for the way things happened. I was in a messed up place in my marriage and an even more messed up place in my mind. I was doing a lot of drugs, and that didn't help the situation. I suspected that Ron was crossing the line, and I failed to protect you. I didn't want to think that it was true. When I found out that you were pregnant, I knew. I knew, and something broke inside of me. I was so broken. It was easy for me to blame you. I didn't want to see Ron as that person. But now, I'm forced to understand exactly who he is—who he has been all along. My baby! He touched my baby!"

I found it hard to comprehend the words that had been spoken. Ron wasn't a good man, a fact that was evidenced by the histories that Sharon and I had shared with him. And even though I tried to recognize the signs with Cassidy, I wanted to believe that Ron could exercise enough restraint to avoid touching her.

A large part of me was proud of Cassidy. Even with the limitations of her abilities, she had managed to stand up for herself enough to make sure that Ron paid for what he had done to all of us. As a woman with a fully functioning mind, I had found it difficult to do that. I addressed Mom, in an attempt to calm her. "I'm glad Cassidy told you. At least you understand who he is now." Mom didn't speak. I called her name, believing that the call had been dropped. "Mom? Are you there Mom?"

I thought that I was shocked by the initial revelation. I couldn't have foreseen that the additions to the story would be even more troubling. Mom spoke. I haven't ever been able to forget her voice as she said the words. "Shelonda, Cassidy didn't tell me that Ron was touching her. I found out in a way that left no questions unanswered." Mom told me that two days prior, she had left work early, as she wasn't feeling well. Upon entering the house, she'd heard Cassidy screaming. Accustomed to Cassidy's tantrums, Mom approached her bedroom, prepared to tell her to keep it down. But when she opened the bedroom door, she'd found that Ron was forcefully raping Cassidy on her bed.

I started seeing red as I replayed the scenario in my mind. I remembered how I felt when Ron used to rape me. That was one of the darkest times in my life. Even being so, I was 16 when things were at their worst. While I was too young to have dealt with where life had taken me, I was strong. I was of sound mind, and I was able to play the game with Ron. But Cassidy was different. Not only did Cassidy lack in understanding, but she was pure. I thought about Ron violating her, and it brought tears to my eyes. Knowing Mom, Cassidy still had cartoon sheets and curtains. How, as a grown man, do you reconcile being aroused by someone who sleeps on Powerpuff Girls sheets? It was incomprehensible.

I hated Ron more than I ever thought I could hate anyone. And trust me, I had plenty of hate in my heart. How dare he take something so innocent and taint it forever? How dare he hurt her in a way that would change her entire outlook on the world? How dare he make her afraid in the one place that should have provided comfort for her? HOW DARE HE?

Somehow, it felt different than when he had done it to me. I wasn't his biological child. That didn't make it ok, but you'd think that he'd feel more protective of his own flesh and blood. But then again, I couldn't forget that he had molested Sharon as well. She was biologically related to Ron, and he still hadn't cared enough to avoid hurting her. Why did I assume that he wouldn't hurt Cassidy? Everyone failed. Sharon's mother failed her. Mom failed me. And when it came down to it, I shouldn't have ever trusted Mom to protect Cassidy. I failed her.

# Chapter 10

## ::::Unmet Obligations—Part 2::::

*T*he whole thing angered and saddened me. And as a result, a part of me reconnected with the love that I had for Mom. We were attached in the way that some Siamese twins are connected—by a small sliver of skin. Cassidy was that sliver of skin. Mom and I had connected as a result of our joint hurt over Cassidy's predicament. And even though Mom had done something that was extremely hurtful to me, I was happy that she had done right by Cassidy. That's what mattered to me. By that point in time, I was far removed from much of the hurt associated with our relationship—or lack thereof. But just as I was falling into my cycle of undeserved forgiveness, Mom helped me to put my feelings back into perspective. She interrupted my thoughts.

"Londa, I need you to do something for me. I know it's a lot to ask, but I need you. I can't deal with all of this right now. I need you to take Cassidy for a while. I'm extremely stressed out, and I don't want to turn to drugs. Plus, with Ron being gone, I can't really afford to take care of her on my own. I've heard that you're doing quite well. I think that you're in a much better position to take care of her than I am."

I immediately jumped out of affection mode. While I had initially been sucked in by Mom's display of emotion, I was suddenly faced with the realization that Mom was participating in her usual antics. I was simultaneously hurt and angry. One thing that I was very much aware of was Mom's work ethic. She was a subpar mother at best, but I never doubted her ability to financially provide for Cassidy. Additionally, Ron hadn't ever contributed much to the household's finances. Those factors taken into account, I couldn't help but to arrive at an inevitable conclusion. Mom was more than capable of taking care of Cassidy. Her request had alerted me to the fact that she had no desire to do so.

Remembering things about our joint history, I realized something about Mom. Ron's love was her primary objective. I went back to when I found out that Mom was pregnant with Cassidy. I remembered the pride that she had in giving Ron a legitimate child of his own. I remembered how she adored Cassidy in the hospital before we realized that she was developmentally delayed. I remembered Mom's inability to protect me. But even more impactful, was why. Mom had failed to protect me because she had more of a vested interest in keeping her relationship with Ron intact. That was the hardcore truth.

A lot of things came into perspective. Mom was asking me to take Cassidy because she had outgrown her need for her. Cassidy was no longer the tie that bound Mom and Ron together. She was damaged goods. As far as Mom was concerned, Cassidy was representative of Ron's indiscretions. Cassidy was a carbon copy of Ron. Everyone always talked about how much she resembled him. Knowing Mom, I couldn't imagine that she could look at Cassidy and not draw a mental reference to him. I wanted to be wrong, but I knew I wasn't. That's who Mom was, and that's how she operated.

I was suddenly very angry and overcome with emotion. I addressed Mom in a way that I hadn't ever imagined that I would. I was always very respectful to her, even when I had no justifiable reason to be. But that day? On that day, I found it impossible to quell my desire to tell Mom exactly what was on my mind. I listened to her logic, and then I delivered a response that she should have received years prior.

"Mom, I've listened to everything that you've said, and I have a personal connection to what happened to Cassidy. How could I not? I dealt with Ron's abuse for years. The one thing that stopped me from coming forward was the realization that I likely would not be believed. I knew that I would be made to feel that my abuse was the result of me being "too grown" or "doing too much". Do you understand how hard it was to realize that I blamed myself for what happened, and you knew the whole time? Do you realize how hard it was to watch you, the one person who had an obligation to me, tell me that you wished death upon me and everything that was connected to me? Do you know how hard it was for me to abort my baby, knowing that I could have avoided that heartache if you had done right by me as a mother? Of course you don't know, because you haven't ever thought past what was convenient for you. So no, I will not take Cassidy. I absolutely feel that I can love her more than you will ever have the ability to, but I WILL NOT give you the benefit of being able to dismiss her for your convenience. Cassidy doesn't have the ability to understand who you are, a fact that I am grateful for. I'm glad that she doesn't understand that she has been a pawn in your pathetic game. But there's one thing that I'm aware of. You WILL make sure that she has what she needs and wants. And since she doesn't have the capacity to express the need for anything on an emotional level, I'm completely comfortable with the fact that she will be ok with you—since Ron has been taken out of the equation, of course."

I didn't know what to expect from Mom, as I hadn't ever challenged her. But her rebuttal made me understand that I'd had an adequate interpretation of who I was dealing with—as much as I wanted to be wrong. Mom addressed me. "Londa, are you sure that this is the position you want to take on this? Think back to your Grandma. She would want you to do the right thing."

I thought back to Grandma. She would, indeed, want me to do the right thing. Grandma wouldn't have turned either of us away, regardless of the situation. But having Mom play the Grandma card infuriated me, and I couldn't resist the urge to tell her so. I lashed out at her. "Mom, you have some nerve. How dare you bring Grandma into this? The Lord should strike you down for even mentioning her name." Before I could really dig into her, Mom opened a box containing the answers that I had been seeking for the entirety of life. She also made me aware that my thinking had been completely on base. She confirmed everything that I felt was true. Mom paused, then addressed me.

"You wanna play this game Londa? Well, let's go. For as smart as you think you are, there are so many things that you don't know. In telling them now, I understand that they will hurt you, but you asked for it. I know you think I don't understand how you feel, but nothing could be further from the truth. I was molested by an older family friend, which resulted in your conception. No one believed me. I wanted to have an abortion, but your Grandma talked me out of it. She told me that she would take over as your primary caretaker if I decided against the abortion. But after your birth, she failed to uphold her end of the bargain. She insisted that I be a full-time mother to you. She let me down, and I haven't ever forgiven her for that. She created a set of circumstances that forced me to look at you every day, the result of something that was so hurtful. I hated men after that point. I went years without the desire to date. And then, came Ron. I fell in love with him, after all the ill feelings that I had towards men. I wanted to leave you with your Grandma, but Ron insisted that I bring you along. Look how that turned out for me. You destroyed everything! And now, this. Cassidy gives me the same feelings that I had when I was forced to keep you. I know that's not right, but that's how I feel. I don't want to be her mother. I've never wanted to be anyone's mother. Your grandma forced me to be a mother to you, and Ron forced me to be a mother to Cassidy. Given the situation, I don't think that he is in a position to require such anymore. Yes, I can provide for her, but I don't think I can love her the way that I should. She's a piece of Ron, and I hate that. So, I have to present you with an ultimatum, because it's the only card that I have left to play. I know how you feel about your sister. I have allowed you to have a relationship with her because I know the situation between you and Ron wasn't entirely your fault. But if you decide not to take primary custody of Cassidy, understand that things will change. If you decide not to take her, you will not have access to her. I will put her in a home and make sure that you won't be allowed to visit her without my approval. Let me tell you now that I will not grant you permission."

I thought long and hard about my options. I loved Cassidy, and I certainly felt that she would be better off with me than in any institution. But the more I thought about it, I really wasn't in a position to be a primary caretaker for Cassidy. My life was all over the place, and I couldn't ensure that I was going to be in the right places at the right times. I didn't have a life that was conducive to being a parent to a ten year old. It sounds bad to say, but it just wasn't convenient for me. That's unfortunate, but those were my thoughts at the time.

I asked to speak to Cassidy. Surprisingly, Mom allowed me to do so. I told Cassidy that I loved her, and I promised that I would always be there if I understood that she needed me. I told Mom that she had to do what she had to do. I didn't want Cassidy to go into the system, but I refused to pause my life so Mom could be free. She didn't deserve to be free. She deserved to live with the hardship of reflection. She deserved to see Cassidy every day, knowing that she was the product of the relationship that caused her to betray me and Grandma. She deserved it all!

I hung up with Mom that day, with the fear that she was going to put Cassidy into an institution. I didn't think I would ever hear from either of them again. I knew I owed it to Cassidy to do better, but I didn't. I did what was best for me, at the expense of Cassidy's well-being. I went out of my way to spite Mom, also at the expense of Cassidy's well-being. I felt awful, and I cried the day away. I walked away from Cassidy, saddened over all of my unmet obligations.

# Chapter 11

## :::::I Loved That:::::

$I$ was truly saddened by the "loss" of Cassidy. I guess it was more about the way things had happened. I was previously ok with things being as they were, as I hadn't ever had the expectation of having Cassidy with me. But knowing that I failed to take advantage of the opportunity to take her weighed heavily upon me. The biggest part of me knew that I should have taken Cassidy. But my life really did move too swiftly. I knew it was selfish on my behalf, but my life would change with the addition of Cassidy. I didn't want my life to change. But life did change—for the better and for the worse.

I continued to work at the gas station—when I wanted to. But outside of that, being Antoni❖'s girlfriend was my fulltime job. There were a few things that I had lost in my pursuit of Antoni❖, but I wasn't in the business of crying over spilled milk. Besides, what I experienced with him far surpassed my desire to hold on to most things. Cassidy was the only exception.

You may be wondering why I was so in love with Antoni❖— especially because of the baggage that came along with him. Sure, he bought me things, but anyone could have bought me things. He took me places, but anyone could have taken me places. We had great sex. I could have gotten that from numerous places as well. I could have gotten all of those things from someone else, but it wouldn't have been the same. No one could have been what Antoni❖ was at that time. He had the ability to make anyone feel as if they were the only person in the world. I loved that.

For example, when I was working at the salon, I had been around Antoni✂ and Sharon on several occasions. Sharon—a woman who Antoni✂ obviously loved. Yet, he still managed to make me feel special in her presence. No, he didn't kiss me or hold my hand. But he catered to me. He showed me that I mattered.

I remember times when he brought food to the salon, fully aware that Sharon was there as well. Yeah, he brought food for both of us, but he sat and talked with me. He ate with me. He looked into my eyes as he spoke to me. He told me that he loved me when we parted company. I never felt as if I were "second".

And I had ALL of his attention otherwise. Antoni✂ refused to entertain Peaches and Cream when I was around. There were several times when one of them would knock on the door when Antoni✂ and I were in his office. Antoni✂ would allow them to enter, but only to tell them that their company wasn't desired. And when we were together as a group, Antoni✂ didn't allow them to speak while I was speaking. At first, he would angrily ask, "You don't hear her talking?" But after a while, it was sufficient for him to shoot them a glance. The look was universally accepted as a request to be quiet—a request that was always honored.

I often wondered if Antoni✂ was abusive to Peaches and Cream outside of my presence. I certainly remembered seeing him choke Cream and throw her onto the floor. If I have to be honest, it bothered me. I had previously been abused, and the thought of them experiencing that was hurtful to me. I would even stick up for them by saying that it was ok. But as Antoni✂ explained, everyone had a place. Our world only operated properly because everyone stayed in line. He explained that to me in front of Peaches and Cream. I was saddened and embarrassed for them.

But it wasn't me, and what Antoni❖ said was true. That was the nature of the world that we lived in, and that's how everything stayed in place.

I can't blame anyone who views those things as disrespectful. Honestly, they were. But at the time, I felt that Antoni❖ was showing me where I fell in his value system. I was in love with him. He was showing me that he was in love with me as well. He promised to show me where I stood with him, and he did. So, I took it all in, and I accepted everyone for where they fell in the system. I no longer cared about the look of it all.

In spite of the fact that I lived fairly close to Sharon, Antoni❖ didn't hide me, and I didn't try to be hidden. As far as I was concerned, if Antoni❖ wanted her to be more relevant, she would have been. It was easy to disregard her existence. And I did. I got comfortable with Antoni❖ and the life that he provided for me. What is the life of which I speak? Let me explain.

I've told you that Antoni❖ did a lot for me. But it was more than that. Antoni❖ exhibited a level of attention to detail that most people would fail to maintain—specifically over a long period of time. It was an unusual phenomenon. He was extremely intense about anything to which he was attached.

Antoni❖ purchased a car for me. It was my dream car, a fact that Antoni❖ was very much aware of. It's easy to pay attention long enough to see the surface of what someone likes. But it was deeper than that with Antoni❖. No detail went unnoticed. Antoni❖ didn't just purchase the car, but he purchased it in the exact color I wanted. He purchased it with the exact specifications that I wanted for the interior. And he took care of it in the same way that he took care of me. I never had to remember to get an oil change. Antoni❖ took care of that. I never had to wash it or vacuum it. Antoni❖ took care of that as well.

Antoni⁑ didn't pay for the maintenance, like he paid for most things. He did the work himself. As he explained it, there were things that had to be nurtured personally because they were too important to entrust to anyone else. Antoni⁑ told me that he would always handle my affairs hands on because he wanted anything tied to me to be kept to his standards. According to Antoni⁑, my car was an extension of me. Therefore, it had to be treated properly. I was an extension of him, so I had to be treated properly as well.

Antoni⁑ told me that he'd refused to allow anyone else to sleep with me because no one would be able to please me the way that he could. Although he said it with the utmost sincerity and absolute conviction, it was laughable. He really pretended that my monogamy wasn't self-serving on his behalf. But that's who Antoni⁑ was, and that's who I allowed him to be. I didn't want anyone else. I didn't think that there was anyone else that could take care of me in the way that Antoni⁑ did. I was happy to live in that fairy tale with him.

And just as Antoni⁑ was attentive in material things, he was also attentive in experiences. I've mentioned that we went to Hawaii. Our trip was absolutely amazing, from start to finish. I hadn't ever been on a trip that was on that level. I hadn't even been on a plane prior to that point. Twelve years my senior, Antoni⁑ had experienced much more and insisted on making all of the arrangements. That was easier for me, so I allowed him to do so. A couple of days prior to the trip, Antoni⁑ asked me to clear my schedule. I did as he requested.

Antoni⁑ picked me up early one morning. He asked if he could make a decision for me. I agreed to his request. Without the benefit of me knowing where we were going, Antoni⁑ drove for four hours before we arrived at a salon. We drove four hours for me to get my hair done, I asked. "I could have gotten my hair done anywhere." "You could have, but they are the best. You are the best, and you deserve the best." That's what Antoni❖ said to me.

We walked into the salon. Two African women welcomed me and told me that they would take good care of me. Both women simultaneously braided my hair. Antoni❖ sat with me the entire time, only leaving to retrieve pain meds for the headache that I'd received as a result of my service. Typically an eight hour job, the women finished my hair in just over three. Not only was it fast, but it was beautiful. And Antoni❖ was right. By my standards at the time, they were the absolute best. Antoni❖ took me home and spent the rest of the day with me.

He arrived early the next morning. Once again, I had no idea where we were headed. I trusted Antoni❖ and followed him blindly. Again, we arrived at a salon that was hours away. I didn't ask any questions that day. I followed him inside. Opposed to a hair salon, we were at a nail salon.

Antoni❖ asked if he could choose my service, and I allowed him to do so. He chose a garra rufa pedicure. Small fish swam around, nibbling away any dead skin cells that may have been present on my feet. The result? My feet were as soft as a baby's bottom. Of course, it prompted a conversation about interspecies and mutually beneficial animal relationships. But I have to be honest, I didn't expect anything different.

Afterwards, Antoni❖ insisted that I also get a manicure, even though I had gotten my nails done earlier in the week. I already knew that he would choose a French manicure. I wasn't a fan of French manicures, but I had already told Antoni❖ that I would allow him to choose for me. In the end, I realized that he had amazing taste. My nails were beautiful. I fell in love with them and have worn my nails that way ever since.

But knowing Antoni❥, I knew that there was a method to the madness. I inquired, of course. I asked Antoni❥ why he had an attachment to French manicures. I expected an elaborate animal reference, but Antoni❥'s answer was simple. Yeah, Antoni❥'s answer was simple.

"Sometimes, less is more. Your strength is in the fact that you are beautifully understated. Don't ever let your things speak so loudly that people can't hear what you have to say."

That was the thing about Antoni❥. As Grandma would say, he went around his elbow to get to his thumb. I always knew exactly what Antoni❥ meant. But he usually insisted on taking the long route around every conversation. Antoni❥ didn't like nail art, as he thought it was ghetto. For anyone else, it would have been sufficient to just say that. But Antoni❥ always worded things in the most complex of ways. He was like a writer of fables. There was always something to be learned. I both loved and hated that about him.

I was at the nail salon for hours. Antoni❥ stayed with me for the entire duration of my visit, only leaving to retrieve food for me. Upon his return, Antoni❥ spoon fed me. Knowing that I had gotten my nails done, he didn't want me to blemish the paint. He literally sat beside me and put the food inside of my mouth. He was very catering in that way. Antoni❥ took me home and spent the rest of the day with me.

On the third day, Antoni❥ took me shopping. Although most men get annoyed with the process, Antoni❥ never did. He patiently waited as I went from store to store, ever so indecisively. He never seemed to mind though. Antoni❥ was the most patient man that I knew. I loved that about him.

And finally, it was time for our vacation. I was content just to be going to Hawaii. But that wasn't enough for Antoni❥. He capitalized on the opportunity to make it memorable. Everything was designed to be comfortable and enjoyable for me.

Hawaii was amazing! From the moment we boarded the plane, Antoni❣ went above and beyond. My very first plane ride was first class. I was nervous about the turbulence. Antoni❣ held my hand until it was over. After making sure that I was comfortable, Antoni❣ ordered breakfast for me. Bacon that was a little too soft, eggs that were a little too cheesy, and grits with sugar, opposed to butter and pepper—just as I would have ordered for myself.

When we landed, we didn't have to wait around for transportation like many of the other passengers. Antoni❣ had arranged everything in advance. We arrived at a beautiful hotel suite that was right on the water. I was excited about being in Hawaii, but Antoni❣ insisted that we take a nap. He wanted to make sure that I was well rested for what the night had in store for me.

Not only was the nap appreciated, but certainly well needed. Antoni❣ and I spent the entire day partying and the entire night having sex. And it wasn't just any kind of sex. It was THE BEST sex. Antoni❣ and I had sex on the beach, sex on the balcony, and sex in the water. We had sex EVERYWHERE! It was amazing! You would think that it would get old, but it didn't. Sex with Antoni❣ never got old. We spent the entire week that way, and I never tired of him. It seemed that he never tired of me. I never wished I was anywhere else.

When we returned, I expected Antoni❣ to take a break from me. I had to be honest with myself about our situation. Antoni❣ had businesses that he needed to attend to, but I also knew that he had other women. I thought back to when Antoni❣ and Sharon returned from Jamaica. Antoni❣ had immediately started "playing make up" with me. I expected that he would have to make up the time with his other women upon our return. But that was not to be the case. Antoni✱ came home with me, disregarding any and everything else that needed to be done.

And that's how we lived from that point forward. If Antoni✱ needed to be somewhere, he expected me to accompany him. If I couldn't accompany him, he expected me to be immediately available upon his return. I was more than happy to oblige.

Many won't understand that level of attachment. But, imagine being with someone with Antoni✱'s lifestyle. Can you imagine how many women wanted to be in my shoes? Imagine knowing that he had a million other things to do, yet, he always chose you. And it wasn't JUST that he chose me. KEN had chosen me as well. But Antoni✱ chose me without me having to hurt. I didn't have to discover his indiscretions and ask him to choose me. He did so of his own free will, and he made me feel that it was his pleasure to do so. That was the blessing and the curse of being with someone like Antoni✱. His love was thick and powerful, and he freely surrounded me with it. And I loved him, so I breathed it in until I choked. I loved everything about him.

# Chapter 12

## ::::He Messed Up::::

*I* took full advantage of being more accessible to Antoni❦. It was a bumpy road at times, but I was along for the ride. By now, you probably know that Antoni❦ wasn't a straight arrow. He had his hands in a lot of things, many of which were illegal. I was very much aware of that fact, as I worked his books. But that wasn't my business, and I didn't ask questions. As Antoni❦ stated, everything worked out in our world because everyone stayed in place and did what they were supposed to do. I stayed in my place and did what I was supposed to do. I guess Antoni❦ forgot that there were things that he had to do as well.

Very few situations last forever—specifically not ones with that much illegal content. But my young mind believed that Antoni❦ and I could continue on that way forever—being in love and benefiting from the businesses. Things were good. But everything is subject to change. We were all about to learn that the hard way.

Our lives got turned upside down in 2001. The events that took place set the stage for a million things that I still wish I could take back. I was 21, and Antoni❦ and I were on top of the world. I became more involved in the day to day operations at the club, and I excelled at learning the ropes. Things were good. Actually, things were great! But the life usually catches up with you, and Antoni❦ and I were not exempt.

I came home from work one night to find Antoni❦ waiting on my sofa. That wasn't unusual. Antoni❦ had a key and pretty much came and went as he pleased. But that night, something was different. The look on his face told me that something was terribly wrong. I sat beside Antoni❦

and asked him what was going on. Baby, I have some bad news, he said. A lump immediately formed in my throat. I had the same feeling that I had on the day Mom tried to kill herself and when she told me that Ron had raped Cassidy.

Antoni❧ buried his face in his hands and told me that he had messed up. He told me that he had gone to his probation office and was surprised with a new officer and a drug test. Just a little tidbit of info: Antoni❧ was on probation, and he had to visit his probation officer monthly. Antoni❧ was a heavy marijuana smoker, and his urine was always dirty. But because it was his way, he was known to pay his probation officer to not submit the actual results. It was a plan that worked out well.....until it didn't.

Apparently, Antoni❧'s probation officer had taken another position and was no longer assigned to him—information that would have been useful prior to his arrival. Long story short, Antoni❧ was unable to pass the drug test. The new probation officer wasn't impressed by him, and she expressed as much. She explained to him that she would be submitting paperwork in reference to his probation violation.

Does that mean you're going to prison, I asked. Antoni❧ shook his head to signal that he would probably be going to prison. How long can they give you for that, I asked. He told me that the judge would make that decision, but he didn't expect a favorable outcome.

I was crushed. I flashed back to the situation with KEN. I couldn't believe that it was happening again. I immediately started to cry. Antoni❧ started to cry as well. A part of me broke inside. I had fought so hard for Antoni❧, and I was about to lose him. But the look on his face told me that his fear was deeper than incarceration. I stood in front of Antoni❧ and cupped his chin in my hand. I saw the apprehension in his eyes, and it caused me to talk myself into a corner. I collected myself enough to address him.

"Baby, I see the fear in your eyes, and I'm scared too. There are so many things that you have failed to share with me, and I've tried to be understanding about that. I can only assume that you have done so for my benefit. But we're past that point now. You're not going to prison by yourself. I'm going to have to serve this time with you. Not only that, but I'm a part of you. Isn't that what you said? You have to let me know everything that we're facing. Whatever it is, we'll get through it together. Baby what do you need from me?"

It seemed that my words were enough to assuage him. Antonie put his arms around my waist. He wiped my tears away, even though his face was saturated with his own. He smiled. It was one of those smiles that was laced with a little bit of sadness. We had a conversation that I never thought I'd have to participate in. Antonie started.

"Him: Do you love me Little Girl?

Me: You know I do.

Him: Tell me you love me.

Me: I love you Baby.

Him: Can I trust you?

Me: You know you can.

Him: This is serious Little Girl. I need you to promise me.

Me: Baby, you can trust me with your life. I promise.

Him: I'm gonna have to.

Me: Have to what?

Him: Trust you with my life."

Antoni❖ told me that he was about to trust me in a way that he hadn't ever trusted anyone else. "Promise me you got me Baby". That's what he said. I promised Antoni❖ that I'd have his back through it all. "Promise me that you won't have me out here looking crazy". Again, I promised. Antoni❖ asked me to have a seat. I did as he requested.

I knew that Antoni❖ was involved in some shady situations, but what he told me blew me away. Antoni❖ told me that he had several businesses, all of which were front companies for his massive drug empire. I wasn't surprised that Antoni❖ was involved with drugs, but I wasn't aware that he had so many things going on, or that his operation was so large. That explained why he seemed to always be in demand. He was being stretched in a million different directions.

Although I knew that he didn't owe it to me, a part of me was bothered that Antoni❖ hadn't taken the time to expose me to the other parts of his life. It was as if he kept me in the one small box in which he felt I would fit. It saddened me a little, but it wasn't the time for me to cry over the sting to my ego. The situation was bigger than me.

Antoni❖ told me that he trusted me, and he needed me to take over while he was away. He told me that he was aware that it was a huge undertaking, but it couldn't be entrusted to just anyone. He referenced the many conversations where he explained how things that matter must be treated differently. Antoni❖ took my hand and addressed me.

"This is serious Little Girl. This ain't pushing paper and moving numbers around. People die when they find themselves on the wrong side of this business. You're good with numbers, and you got a good head on your shoulders. But it's bigger than that. You have to be the boss that I know you can be. You gotta stand up to the world like you stand up to me. There are a lot of rules to this game, but if you follow 'em, you'll be fine. Can I trust you to do this for me Little Girl?"

Antoni told me that he didn't know when he would be picked up, but he would give me all of the information that was needed before that point in time. I took a moment to take in everything that Antoni said. A couple of things jumped out at me.

First and foremost, Antoni told me that he was about to trust me in a way that he hadn't trusted anyone. A part of me was impressed and intrigued. I was the newest of "Antoni's girls". There was a lot to be said about the fact that he was willing to trust me, opposed to everyone else.

There was no expectation that Antoni would trust Cream and Peaches to that degree. Our conversations had cued me in to the fact that they had proven themselves unworthy. They were shrimp. But Sharon was different. In spite of the fact that I had taken Sharon's place, I was aware that Antoni held her in very high regards. By his own admission, Antoni saw Sharon very differently than he saw Peaches and Cream.

Sharon had been successfully running her salon for years, and it was obvious that she had a good head for business. So why hadn't Antoni gone to her? Maybe he thought that she would be too busy to handle her own business and his as well. Maybe, he knew that she would be opposed to taking over. If the latter was true, I had to consider why that may have been.

Maybe Sharon would have declined for a valid reason. I didn't know everything about Antoni's businesses, but it was obvious that there would be some risks involved. While it was easy for me to say the words that provided Antoni with some comfort, I had to consider the fact that the task would be a larger undertaking than he'd mentioned.

But I had already given Antoni my word. And the fact of the matter is, there was no way that I was going to allow any of the other women to be that person for him. I had worked hard to be everything that none of the others could be, and I wasn't about to let that go. I promised Antonio that I would do what I had to do to keep things intact. My mind flashed back to KEN and our promise. Once again, a promise was about to take me to a place that I never should have gone. But that would happen much later.

I stood and positioned myself between Antonio's legs. I started removing my clothes. What are you doing, he asked. I told him that we needed to take advantage of every moment that we had available. Antonio smiled, a genuine smile. "I'm never gonna love anybody else the way I love you." That's what he said to me. I smiled as well.

Antonio picked me up and carried me to my bedroom. I loved when he did that. Antonio was big and strong. He made me feel secure and protected. I couldn't imagine how life would be without him. We made love multiple times that night. We both knew that we were on borrowed time.

# Chapter 13

## ꞉꞉꞉꞉Learning The Ropes꞉꞉꞉꞉

The next day, we went to Antonio's lawyer. I read the sign as we parked in front. The Law Office of David L Herkowitz, Esq. His office was exquisite and impeccably designed. I remember wondering how much Antonio was paying him. That level of luxury certainly didn't come cheap.

Antonio signed all of his businesses over to me and made me the executor of his estate. He even made me the beneficiary of his life insurance policies. That's when things started to get real for me. Antonio was serious about getting everything in order. If I have to be honest, it made me worry a little more. It was as if Antonio didn't think he would make it out of prison. Like he assumed that I would mess things up so much that he would be murdered as a result. That's enough to scare anyone—especially someone with no point of reference to the subject at hand. But it was too late to turn around. It was happening.

After signing everything over, Antonio started the process of exposing me to all of the businesses. I knew everything there was to know about the strip club. I immaculately kept his books. I even knew how to order everything that was needed and handle payroll. Antonio had a few other businesses that pretty much ran the same way. I learned that there was a "me" at each business.

In each case, there was a cute, young girl who managed the paperwork and kept things in line. It was very obvious that the girls didn't like me, and I wondered if Antonio was sleeping with them as well. It seemed that they always smiled before realizing that I was with Antonio.

They weren't ever really receptive towards me, and I made sure to let them know that I noticed. I didn't speak to them, and I allowed my facial expressions to convey my feelings. Neither side had to wonder how the other felt.

I never mentioned my discomfort to Antoni. I knew what he would say, and I was in no mood for his theatrical breakdown of fabled logic. "If you're not ready to be hated, you're not ready to be successful." That's exactly what Antoni would have said. Besides, I didn't have the time to stress about that. If they were getting any time at all, it was certainly the leftovers that I had allowed them to have. Antoni and I were locked in. And if I had to be honest, I knew I would be firing them as soon as Antoni went away. That was locked in as well.

I watched everything closely and took everything in. Running the businesses would be easy. Without the distraction of Antoni, I could easily juggle them and make things flow a little more easily. While handling the books, I had thought of so many ways to improve the operation. However, saying so would have required that I step on Antoni's toes. But with him being gone, there would be no one to object to my way of doing things. I wasn't concerned about that part of it. The other business, however, would be a struggle. The idea of running a drug empire became more and more daunting with each day that passed. I was constantly back and forth about it all.

Thinking back, I always knew that Antoni sold drugs. I was just under the impression that it was on a smaller scale. We didn't discuss it, and he didn't bring it around me. But with his impending incarceration and my imminent takeover, I was forced to dig deep into the life. That made me incredibly nervous. That was Antoni's world. It wasn't mine.

Truthfully, I had no desire to intermingle myself with the wilds of Antoni's illegal life. I agreed to his request to make him feel better, but I knew that I didn't belong there. In fact, I suggested that he pause his drug business until he was released. Antoni❖ laughed while addressing my request. "This isn't a movie Little Girl. You can't just pause it." He told me that it didn't work that way. There were people above and below him, and he couldn't just bow out. He told me that people got killed when expectations weren't met.

I got a sinking feeling in the pit of my stomach. Even with doing everything the right way, anything could happen. And I was thinking about changing everything. I was, again, presented with the thought of Antoni❖ getting killed in prison as a result of me dropping the ball. I couldn't face that. I knew I would have to dig deep. Antoni❖ sensed my apprehension and made me feel better. "You can do this Little Girl. You're stronger than you think." He always knew exactly what to say.

The way Antoni❖ explained things made them seem very simple. I never had to touch or even see the drugs. All I had to do was talk, make deals, pay money, and collect money. It seemed simple enough, and his breakdown made me feel slightly better.

Antoni❖ said that he would introduce me to everyone that I needed to know and give me the rundown on exactly how everything was to go. I was scared. Other than "tweaking" the books, I hadn't really done anything illegal—definitely not anything on that level. But I didn't want Antoni❖ to feel that he couldn't depend on me. I attempted to put my worries aside and take in everything that he told me. I had to make it work.

Many people will wonder why I agreed to take on such an extreme undertaking. Most people wouldn't just agree to become a drug dealer, especially not on such a large scale. But you have to understand something. Antoni❖ had been good to me. According to my perspective at the time, he supplied my wants, needs, and deepest desires. He provided some things that I didn't even know I wanted or needed, and he hadn't ever really expected anything from me. Additionally, I couldn't discredit the fact that I had been more than willing to spend every dime that Antonio accumulated from said drug business. Those were my thoughts at the time. That's what made it easier for me to cross that line.

Antonio made the introductions and let it be known that everyone was to handle things just as they would if they were dealing with him. I could tell the guys respected Antonio. That helped me to feel a little more comfortable. Maybe the respect that they had for Antonio would spill over to me. Deep down, I felt that it would. Antonio wouldn't put me in danger. He loved me too much.

So, I took everything in and prepared to take on my new role. Like I said, there was no turning back. I promised Antonio that he could leave it all in my hands and I wouldn't make him regret it. I agreed to everything that was asked of me. As it turns out, we would both end up regretting that to an immeasurable degree.

# Chapter 14

## ꞉꞉꞉꞉Handling Business꞉꞉꞉꞉

Antoni⁙ brought Peaches in to help me with the drug business. She knew the process like the back of her hand, and Antoni⁙ knew that. And even though I had taken what should have been hers several times over, Peaches agreed to help me with no questions or resistance. Antoni⁙ explained the situation to Peaches and told her that he expected her to do for me what she would have done for him. She agreed. Outside of her presence, Antoni⁙ issued a stern warning. Remember, he said. "Peaches is a shrimp. You have to domesticate her. You have to control what she eats."

I took it all in, but I have to be honest. I didn't understand the partnership between Antoni⁙ and Peaches. They certainly didn't have a clownfish and anemone relationship. It seemed to be more like a killer whale and a sardine. It didn't seem that she was getting anything out of dealing with Antoni⁙, which was strange. He was very generous.

I assumed she was getting SOME money from him, but it obviously hadn't been enough to improve her lifestyle. Peaches was living in the same apartment, driving the same car, and working the same "job" as the day I met her. It seemed that she had every reason to walk away, but she didn't. I wondered why she never felt that she could do better. But in the moment, I was glad that she didn't. I felt more comfortable knowing that I would have someone familiar on my side, even if she was a shrimp.

Two weeks passed before Antoni⁙'s recklessness caught up with him. Antoni⁙ and I went out to see a movie. In typical Antoni⁙ fashion, he took me a movie that made me think a little too much. He chose to take me to see the movie "Blow". Leave it to Antoni❦ to take me to a movie about the rise and fall of a drug kingpin.

After leaving the movie, Antoni❦ was pulled over for not using his turn signal. Of all things, not using a turn signal. I hated that my time with Antoni❦ had been cut short. I wanted as much time with him as I could possibly have. I was sad, but I knew the day would come. He knew it as well. Antoni❦ told me that he loved me and he trusted me with his life. The last thing he said to me was "Don't let the life swallow you up Little Girl". Then, he went away. Just like that, he was gone.

Antoni❦ was scheduled for a bond hearing a week later. The judge set his bail, and it would cost $5,000 to get him out. Antoni❦ had $5,000 many times over, and I was fully prepared to pay it. I thought Antoni❦ would jump at the opportunity to get out of jail, but he instructed me to save the money. He said he would just wait it out until it was time for him to go to court.

A part of me was devastated. I wanted every single second that I could have with him. But the other part of me was impressed. Antoni❦ was willing to stay in jail to make sure that he left me with as much money as possible. He told me that he would rather stay inside than to pull anything from what should have been left to me. That's love, I thought. I loved the way he loved me.

Waiting was the hardest part. I missed Antoni❦, but I was more worried about what was going to happen in the future. I didn't have to handle Antoni❦'s business until he was officially away, and I was on pins and needles waiting the time out. Even though I was terrified, I needed for it to be over either way. It's crazy how perspective on time changes. My entire relationship with Antoni❦ seemed to pass in the blink of an eye. But waiting for his court date seemed to take forever. I guess it's true what they say, time flies when you're having fun.

When it was all said and done, the judge gave Antoni℈ three years for his probation violation. Although I was saddened that he had received that much time, I was relieved that we had some finality. I was relieved that the wait was over. All we had to do was count down until his release. Antoni℈ receiving his time did, however, solidify my position. Everything was handed over to me on the day that he was sentenced. I didn't have anyone else to depend on. I had to handle business— legitimate and otherwise.

Peaches was a godsend in the first few weeks. As I said before, she knew the business like the back of her hand. She knew how to look the part, and she made me look credible. I got the hang of things pretty quickly. Antoni℈ was right. All I had to do was talk, make deals, pay money, and collect money. The minute details took care of themselves. I knew what was happening, and I knew who was making it happen. I didn't bother with the details, and everything worked out just as Antoni℈ said it would. True to his word, Antoni℈ had set everything up perfectly.

I fired Antoni℈'s girls from the other businesses and took over the day to day operations. I did them a solid, however. I gave them a small severance package. It was certainly more than they deserved, and more than they would have gotten in any other situation. They hated me, and I didn't care much for them either. Under any other set of circumstances, they would have walked away with nothing. I only looked out for them because I remembered being broke and trying to figure it all out. In spite of my dislike for them, I had no desire to create a situation of struggle. But they had to go. They no longer had a place there.

I dug deep into their "keeping" of the businesses. The other girls definitely weren't as sharp as I was. And after seeing their handiwork, I was even happier that I had fired them. I didn't understand how the businesses had sustained as long as they did. I made sure that everything was up to par though. I wanted to make sure that Antoni❣ would be happy with what he came home to.

I did exactly what I felt was owed to Antoni❣. I took care of his business, visited weekly, and sent him money. I respected him in the same way that I did when he was home. A few of the guys expressed an interest in something romantic, but I was sure to shut it down. Most of them were Antoni❣'s goons. They were the help. I made sure they respected me, and I made sure they respected Antoni❣. I promised Antoni❣ that I wouldn't do anything that would have him looking crazy in the streets—a promise that I took very seriously. I kept Antoni❣ informed about everything, and I even looked out for Cream and Peaches in the same way that he did. I couldn't believe how easy it was.

The money came in fast and hard. And while I had initially felt indebted to Antoni❣, a couple of things started to change by month two. For the first time, I understood how Antoni❣ was able to afford four girlfriends. The money was rolling in faster than I could keep up with. Also, for the first time, I started to feel shortchanged by Antoni❣. I saw what he was pulling in versus what he was putting out. I felt that Antoni❣ could have invested more into me, a thought that weighed heavily upon me.

While I was doing the math on how I was going to afford a college education, Antoni❣ could have paid my tuition multiple times over. I thought about the fact that he had gotten my breasts done, but he hadn't volunteered to help when I had to replace my roof due to a leak. I started to question my position in Antoni❣'s value system. It wasn't necessarily WHERE I fell that bothered me. My issue was WHY I was in that place.

In my mind, the answer was fairly simple. Antoni❣ did things for me that made him look good. I was his trophy. The idea of me looked good. I was young, pretty, and I spoke well. I owned my own house. I wasn't "hood" like Cream and Peaches. I didn't do drugs. I wasn't a shrimp. I wasn't a prude like Sharon. I was sexually adventurous. I was smart. I worked the books. I made Antoni❖ look good.

Don't get me wrong, I acknowledge where I'd benefited in the situation. Antoni❖ had done a lot for me, and he was exactly what I wanted and needed at the time. When I started dealing with him, I was fresh out of my situation with KEN. Antoni❖ was a breath of fresh air because he exposed me to different things. KEN was a young boy, and I was impressed by the prospect of being with a man. Antoni❖ showed me bigger and better things. He showed me, what I felt were, the finer things and elevated me sexually. I wasn't in denial about his contributions to my life.

But at the same time, I was aware that Antoni❖ did a lot for me that was for his benefit as well. I wondered if he had ever done anything SOLELY for my benefit. Yet, there I was. I was 21 years old, an academic scholar, raised in church, and selling drugs. I hadn't come to that point on my own accord. I was living that life because Antoni❖ needed me to. I was risking my life and freedom because of a misguided loyalty to him.

Again, I was back and forth about the whole thing. I was aware that I wouldn't have chosen that life for myself. But, if I have to be honest, I loved the money, and I loved being in charge. I loved making moves and knowing that others would follow my lead. I loved the life.

I had always allowed the men in my life to make the decisions, even though I would have been much better off if I had gone my own way. Antoni❖'s incarceration gave me a renewed sense of belief in myself and my abilities. I still loved Antoni❖. I handled his business, visited, and sent money. I didn't do anything that would make him look crazy in the streets. However, I set things up to be more beneficial to me. That was only fair.

Many people might say that I stole from Antoni●. I didn't look at it that way. I simply made things fair. Prior to Antoni●'s incarceration, he incurred the risk, and he reaped the rewards. He gave me what he wanted me to have. Now, being the person who was at risk, I felt slighted by only taking what Antoni● wanted me to have. Antoni● had all the finer things in life. Why shouldn't I also have those things? Why should I only give myself what would allow Antoni● to look good? So, it was settled. I worked the books and took a little off of the top. I fixed up Grandma's house and made sure I "looked the part". Antoni● was none the wiser.

After six months, I no longer had to alter the books. All of the income in the main business accounts was legitimately from business operations. There were tangible worksheets that explained what was coming in and what was going out. Each business also had a sub account, which actually held the proceeds from the drug business. Every so often, I would make deposits into the sub accounts and relate the proceeds to an actual event.

For instance, I would receive $25,000 from the drug sales. The next week, I would throw an event at the club and anticipate a large crowd. All money from the actual event would be deposited into the main account. The $25,000 would be deposited into the sub account, as if it were income from the event. It was perfect, and it worked. It probably would have worked for the entire time that Antoni● was away, but I guess I got too big for my britches, as Grandma would say. Antoni● had set everything up for me. But of course, I wanted more....

# Chapter 15

## ::::A Star Is Born::::

Antoni: had been in jail for a year. For all intents and purposes, he and I were solid. I still handled the businesses like I said I would. I didn't intermingle with the guys. I didn't ruin his credibility in the streets. I didn't give anyone a reason to report back to Antoni:. But that would change, of course.

If I have to be honest, there was no reason for me to have done what I did. I guess the best explanation is that I was seduced by the power. I had more money than I could spend, and certainly more than I had ever had. I didn't need anything more. There often comes a point in life where you have to say "enough is enough". At that time, it seemed that there was never enough. That would be my downfall.

I had the best of everything, but I still wanted more. It wasn't just financial. I wanted the name. I wanted the success. I wanted the accolades. I wanted to prove to everyone else that I could do what I knew I could do.

Antoni:'s businesses were his. And although he had been in jail for an entire year, the success of his businesses was still attributed to him. I made the businesses run smoothly, but Antoni: received all of the praise. Even though I solely created the system of sub accounts and elevated the businesses, it was Antoni: who looked the part. I wasn't ok with that, and I felt that I deserved to be a star in my own right. So, I set the stage for that to happen.

If you remember, Peaches was instrumental in my initial success. I was grateful, and I rewarded her handsomely. Peaches was important because she knew the process and she knew the people. Remember that. It will be important later.

Peaches and I became quite close, even to the point of spending time together outside of the business. While I had initially been very close to Cream, our relationship took a backseat as a result of the time that I was spending with Peaches. Peaches was a sweetheart, and I grew to love her like family. She even purchased matching friendship bracelets for us both. Opposite sides of a broken heart dangled from each bracelet. When put together, they spelled the word "friends".

While not my most expensive piece of jewelry, I cherished it. I hadn't had a lot of female friends in my lifetime, and I loved the closeness that we shared. Peaches wasn't perfect, and I knew that I had to stay on top of her. Antoni❣ had warned me about her on several occasions. But handling the business outside of him, gave me a different perspective.

Antoni❣ and I moved differently, so there were different motives and expectations. Much of the discord that happened was the result of feelings and emotions. Cream and Peaches had beef related to their competition for Antoni❣'s affection. But it was different with us. I wasn't sleeping with the women, and they weren't in love with me. No one had to betray the other to stay in my good graces. Those facts alone made it easier for us to keep things more professional.

There was no competition. I looked out for them, and they did what was expected. Everything flowed so smoothly that I was forced to realize that Antoni❣ was the precipitator of many of the issues. He made them compete. He made us all vie for his attention, with the understanding that there could only be one winner. I broke that apart when Antoni❣ left. We all worked together, and we all won. That wouldn't ever have happened if Antoni❣ was around.

Spending time with Peaches put some other things into perspective as well. I learned quite a bit about her and the relationship that she shared with Antoni❖. I understood why she always said that it wasn't easy for her to just walk away, even though she had every reason to.

Peaches remained consistent in her account of the events. She maintained that she had taken a charge for Antoni❖ and expected to come home to him and a thriving business. What she added to the equation was why she was indebted to Antoni❖ in the first place.

Apparently, Antoni❖ was once running a successful escort business. Cream and Peaches were splitting their time between working at the club and working in the escort business—which made me understand why Antoni❖ had lost respect for them. That's why he had insisted that they were shrimp.

Antoni❖ had a steady stream of customers, and business was going well. Peaches was popular amongst the clients, and she pulled in a lot of money. The flaw in the plan came in the form of something that was as old and universal as time—love.

At that point, Cream had taken over, and Antoni❖ wasn't heavily involved with Peaches. Lonely and in need of companionship, Peaches fell in love with one of the clients. She didn't just fall in love, which was against Antoni❖'s number one rule, but she also broke rule number two—never have unprotected sex. Peaches broke both rules, and the evidence exposed everything.

A while into her "affair", Peaches found out that she was pregnant. Scared and confused, she confided in Cream, who took the information straight to Antoni❖—quickly. She and Cream were competitors. I didn't understand why Peaches trusted Cream to keep the news to herself. Maybe she just needed to get it off of her chest.

Peaches said that Antonio was angry, but he offered her an ultimatum. He told her that she could have the baby and go on her way, or he would pay for an abortion and everything would be square between the two of them. Unsure of the possibility of a relationship with the client, and not 100 percent sure of the baby's paternity, Peaches decided to go ahead with the abortion.

It seemed that the problem was solved until Antonio accompanied Peaches to her appointment and found that she was not only pregnant, but she had herpes as well. Needless to say, that complicated the situation quite a bit. Obviously, Peaches was off the market, which caused Antonio to take a financial loss. But that was the least severe of the issues. A few of the clients tested positive for herpes as well. As a result, no one was willing to "do business" with any of Antonio's girls, and he lost all income related to the escort business.

Peaches told me that Antonio had instructed his goons to teach her a lesson. She was beaten so badly that she had to be hospitalized. Antonio blamed her for the demise of his business, rightfully so. He told her that she would dance for free until he felt that he had been adequately compensated for the income lost by the demise of the escort business. Peaches had long since paid her debt, but she stayed because it was all she knew. Peaches had been in the business since she was 18, and she didn't have experience doing anything else.

Peaches' version of the events cleared some things up for me. It was easier for me to understand why she was at the bottom of the hierarchy, and why she didn't seem to be benefiting from dealing with Antonio. It also helped me to understand some of the discord between Cream and Peaches.

I had no doubt that Cream had spilled the beans to gain favor with Antonio. That's how the system worked. Cream was all about the money, and she didn't mind selling Peaches out to climb the ladder. Cream's betrayal struck a chord with Peaches. For reasons that are incomprehensible to me, she trusted Cream to keep her secrets. Realizing that she had been sold out was hurtful to her.

Peaches also helped me to understand how Sharon had been added to the equation. According to Peaches, Cream and Sharon had "a thing" back in the day. Sharon was having a hard time financially. Cream introduced her to Antoni☂, thinking that they would both just get his money. Of course, things didn't work out that way. Sharon came in and took Cream's spot. That was interesting information.

The crazy thing is, I felt as if I was Sharon's karma. Taking it even further, maybe Cream was Peaches' karma for some act that I wasn't aware of. Cream betrayed Peaches, Sharon betrayed Cream, and I betrayed Sharon. I wondered who would show up to deliver the karma that I'd incurred for my indiscretions. I wondered when my karma would arrive.

Those conversations with Peaches taught me a very valuable lesson about Antoni☂ as well. He was always receptive to something newer and fresher. All of the women had betrayed each other on his account. Each one that arrived was younger and had more to offer. I realized how easily I could be betrayed and replaced. I had to set myself up to be able to maintain when Antoni☂ found the new me—or maybe that's just the excuse I gave myself. Either way, Peaches was willing to help. I decided to start my own operation.

I gave Antoni☂ a rundown of my plan. And while he wasn't sold on the idea, he knew that he couldn't stop me. But because he was Antoni☂, he submitted a set of rules that I was expected to follow. He gave me the rundown when I came to visit.

"Little Girl, ain't nothing I can do from in here, and I know you well enough to know that you're gonna do what you wanna do anyway.

From what I can see, you're handling my business, and I respect you for that. But understand that nothing about that is to change. If you find that you can't manage both, the decision will be very easy for you. Make sure that I come home to what I left, and don't have me looking crazy in the streets. Everything outside of that is your business. Remember what I told you, people get killed when things go awry. I don't ever want you to experience the consequences of things not going according to plans."

I laughed when Antonie gave me the rules. You still think you're somebody, I said. Antonie laughed as well. "You came to ask for permission. I must be." That's what he said, and that's what he meant. I knew that Antonie was serious. And even though I laughed it off, I knew the implications of not following the rules. I governed myself accordingly.

So, the plan was put in motion. Outside of Antonie, Peaches had connections in "the underworld". Based on Peaches' account of the herpes incident and my conversation with Antonie, I decided not to include any of Antonie's resources in my solo venture. I had no desire to be on the receiving end of his goon request.

I was sure to make a clear distinction between my business and Antonie's. I made a business plan, and starting setting everything into motion. Peaches told me what I needed to do, and I told Peaches what she HAD to do. And since I was dealing with people that I didn't know, Peaches suggested that I use a pseudonym instead of my real name.

The story of the names has always been hilarious. I hadn't given that much thought to it, but hearing the details showed me how wrong I had gotten it. Remember, when I initially met Peaches and Cream, I thought that they were a lesbian couple. Amazingly, the situation was an ingenious accident.

Peaches explained to me that Antonie had named her Peaches because of her butt. Apparently, he said that it looked like two big peaches. I tried to figure out the story of Cream's name. She wasn't white, or even close. I gave up and allowed Peaches to tell me the story.

Peaches told me that Antoni⚱ had named her Cream because of one of his favorite songs. It was a rap song by his favorite group, Wu Tang Clan. The song is C.R.E.A.M, aptly titled because it was an acronym for "cash rules everything around me." Also aptly titled, Cream certainly lived up to her name. Her favorite saying was "I'm byte my muney."—Cream-nese for "I'm about my money." Cream was quite avaricious. She was, indeed, about her money. It ruled everything around her.

There was an additional humor related to the names that Antoni⚱ gave the women. While not the biggest fans of each other, Peaches and Cream were always grouped together in conversation. People always referred to them as Peaches and Cream—just like that. I always assumed that they were intentionally grouped together, but it was just a random fluke that everyone ran with.

And without the benefit of the whole story, everyone assumed that they were a team—the team of Peaches and Cream. That couldn't have been further from the truth. They kept the peace at Antoni⚱'s request, but neither of them really cared for the other. It was laughable that Antoni⚱ had, once again, created a set of circumstances that forced them to be merged together. Actually, it was hilarious.

But for as amusing as it was, it was also annoying. Peaches and Cream had names that were sexy and witty. Meanwhile, everyone referred to me as "Little Girl" because Antoni⚱ had set that standard. I don't have to tell you that I wasn't willing to take that lying down. From that moment on, I would be known as Star. I chose that name because Antoni⚱ always told me that I looked like a movie star. It just fit, and I went with it.

Peaches made the calls, and I arranged the meeting details. I used the exact set up that I created for Antoni⁚'s businesses to start my own operation. I took all the money that I had "skimmed" from Antoni⁚ and purchased a bar. I called it Star's Bar. Again, it just fit, and I went with it.

I set the main account and the sub account for the "extra" income. I started on a smaller scale. If the drug thing didn't work out, I would always have legitimate money from the bar. It was a thoughtless process after handling Antoni⁚'s businesses. Things worked out well, possibly too well. I got greedy. Not only did I get greedy, but I got sloppy.

With Antoni⁚'s businesses and my business, I was stretching myself a bit too thin. Since I wasn't willing to let anyone else handle Antoni⁚'s matters, I decided to give Peaches a little more responsibility with my bar—with clear cut rules, of course.

- Peaches was not to be romantically linked to anyone who was involved in our businesses.
- Peaches was not to make any decisions without my approval.
- Peaches was not to do business with anyone who was outside of my approved list.
- Peaches was not to break the rules!

Peaches stopped stripping and came to work for me full-time. I listed her as a manager at the bar so she could have a legitimate stream of income. Peaches hadn't ever held a legitimate job that required her to have a bank account or W-2. I wanted to build her up to the point where she could survive without Antoni⁚ upon his return. She didn't deserve to be indebted to him forever. Nobody deserves that.

Peaches was exactly what I thought she would be. She did exactly what was asked of her, and she never complained. Peaches and I were friends. I thought she was loyal, and I felt that I could trust her. What I didn't take into account was the fact that she was also reckless and impulsive. I forgot that she was a shrimp.

# Chapter 16

## ∷∷∷Angelic Devil∷∷∷

*J*ust so you understand how the situation got so out of control, let me explain some things. First, let me give you a breakdown of the rules that I gave to Peaches. Then I'll give you a breakdown of the business structure, so you'll understand why the rules were so important.

First and foremost, Peaches was not to be involved with any of the men that we did business with. That wasn't because of her past, but because of mine. I had certainly been a fool for love, and hadn't made the best decisions as a result. I didn't want Peaches' judgment to be clouded by a man with an agenda.

Secondly, all decisions were to be approved by me. I trusted Peaches to be loyal, but I didn't trust her to be smart. Even with the best of intentions, I couldn't expect that Peaches would make the same decisions that I would. I couldn't trust that.

Third, Peaches was not to do business with anyone who wasn't on the list that was preapproved by me. If anything went awry, I wanted to have a limited pool of potential perpetrators. That's the only way that I could exercise some control in the situation.

I don't have to tell you that Peaches broke every one of those rules, and the consequences would be detrimental to everyone involved.

Now that you know the rules, let me tell you about the business structure. Antoni: and I both were both Point B's. The Point B people were basically middle men within the cycle. Point A was the holder of the large quantities, and we (Point B) had a contract with them. That's why Antoni☏ had insisted that he couldn't just pause his operation while he was away. He still had to honor his contract. That's why he was so afraid.

Per the routine, the point A would send their connect to us (Point B) with whatever quantities that we'd agreed upon. Upon receipt, we would distribute equal quantities to four separate Point C connections. The process would move in the reverse for the return. The Point C connections would sell their quantities and return a profit to us (Point B). We would collect the profit and use some of it to purchase more from the Point A. Any money that was left over was ours to keep—and there was always plenty left over.

Many people will wonder why the Point A didn't just distribute directly to the Point C. It certainly would have made the process a little easier. But there's something that you have to understand about the business. The Point A people attempted to keep their hands clean at all times. They weren't the average people on the street.

Typically, the Point A only chose to deal with people who they knew to be solid. They had too much to lose. Many of the Point C people were petty hustlers and they couldn't be trusted. Thus, the Point A absolved themselves of liability by only dealing with one unit that they felt they could trust—the Point B.

The Point A wasn't ever to be exposed to the Point C guys. Any indiscretion on behalf of the Point B would be "handled" by the Point A goons. That was very much understood, and we didn't play games with them.

The Point B had a little more liability, specifically me. As a point B, I had to watch out for issues from both sides. The Point A would hold me responsible if I messed up. Additionally, they would hold me responsible if a Point C messed up. I was expected to keep the Point C guys in line and ensure that they respected me in the same way that I respected the Point A. That wasn't easy in the beginning.

First and foremost, I'm a woman. Having a woman in that position was almost unheard of. Many of the men in the business felt that they could easily get over on me. I had to assert myself very early on. Admittedly, I had an ally that most Point B's didn't have—my Point A.

My Point A was named Diablo. Diablo was a filthy rich business man from Colombia. He had an impeccable record and status within the community. He was certainly about his business in all areas. After meeting for the initial time, Diablo insisted that he and I meet periodically to discuss business. That's how it started out, and it remained that way for a while. But a year into our dealings, the tide started to change. What can I say, I broke rule number one. I broke the rule HARD!

Like I said, it was fairly innocent at first. Diablo and I would meet and discuss ways for me to advance—ways for me to expand my operation. But around the end of our first year working together, he began to flirt with me.

Initially, it was just smiling and winking. Then, it progressed to an outright request. Initially, I had no intention of taking it further. But........I did what I had always done. I saw the benefit of dealing with Diablo, and that was enough to tip me over to the other side. Diablo didn't hide his intentions. He presented the quid pro quo straight out of the gate. He was direct and to the point.

"I can see why they call you Star. You certainly shine like one. I'm going to tell you something that I won't ever tell another Point B. You're bigger than this. You have this thing locked down. You need to level up if you're going to stay in this business. I can put you where you need to be, but you have to do a couple of things for me. First of all, you have to replace your Point C guys. I don't like them, and I have a situation in mind that will move you along nicely. I have three women that can out hustle your guys any day. Additionally, we can remove some of the issues related to you dealing with those immature boys. Do you know how impressive that will be? A professional dream team of women is unheard of. You WILL be a STAR! Second, I want you. I'm not going to dance around that. I know about your little boyfriend, but he's of no consequence to me. I know you love him, but you need to understand that he can't do anything for you right now. I place a lot of value in respect, so I won't disrespect your relationship. I assume you will respect mine as well. No strings attached Star. When he comes home, you guys can carry on—assuming you still want him. So, what's it going to be? Can we make these things happen?"

Yep! Just like that. Just like that, I said yes. I said yes without even thinking about it. I didn't think about the potential complications. I didn't think about the blowback. I didn't think about how Antonie would feel if he found out. I just said yes.

The moment the word left my mouth, Diablo got down to business. Give me your phone, he said. I reached into my purse and passed my phone over to him. He inserted a number into my contacts and passed it back over to me. I looked down at my phone. I snickered and addressed him. "Angel? Who's Angel?" He laughed as well. My legal name is Angel, he said. He told me that since he and I were about to get "personal", I should address him by his real name.

I found it laughable that his birth name was Angel, but his cartel name was Diablo—Spanish for devil. Not as funny was the reasoning for his nickname. Apparently, Angel was quite ruthless. While most Point A people relied on their goons, Angel didn't mind getting his hands dirty. He had quite a reputation for handling his business. He was rough, in every single way. He also insisted that I call my Point C guys to let them know that they were no longer needed—while I was right there with him.

Angel was deliberate and to the point. He didn't cut any corners. I did as I was told.

Angel and I had sex that same day. He was soft and gentle. He kissed me the right way. It reminded me of the way that Antonio made love to me, and I felt guilty. But that didn't last long at all. Angel had a way of showing you who he was.

Sex with Angel always started off very sensually. But after I was legitimately aroused, he made sure to let me know that he was in charge. Angel loved rough sex. And when I say rough, I mean rough. Angel loved to pull hair, choke, and spank. Initially, it was uncomfortable. But after a while, I was incredibly turned on by him. He was powerful. He was aggressive. I loved that.

I did whatever he asked, and he upheld his end of the bargain. He set me up with a power team of Point C women, and they were amazing. They were professional and firm. They didn't play games, and I never had to worry about them trying to sleep with me. Just as Angel said, they were perfect. My business jumped in a way that I couldn't ever have imagined. It was amazing, and I rode the wave. All was well, until I forgot to feed Peaches....

# Chapter 17

## ꞉꞉꞉꞉Hungry Lion꞉꞉꞉꞉

*I* often reference conversations that I've had with Antoni꞉ when things go awry. One thing that Antoni꞉ always told me was to pay more attention to what someone has done, opposed to what you expect them to do. He had a way of speaking to me in the way that a father speaks to a child. It was simultaneously amusing and insulting.

But one fact couldn't be disputed. Antoni꞉ was usually correct in his assessment of the situation. In his attempt to get me to understand his feelings about Peaches, Antoni꞉ broke it down to me in this way.

"Let me tell you something Little Girl. Very few things will surprise you if you, expect the worse from everybody—even people who have given you no reason to do so. But understand that you can't ever trust somebody who has crossed you. You can't even trust somebody who you understand has crossed someone else. Your love for a person will not stop them from being who they truly were intended to be. Let's say you're a trainer at a zoo. You may have the best relationship with the lion that no one else can tame. That lion may take a liking to you, and you may feel that you have earned its respect. But understand that if you fail to feed that lion one time, he will eat you. The fact that you wouldn't eat a lion will not be taken into consideration. That lion WILL eat you, because the lion seeks to be full at any cost. That's why you gotta keep your eyes open Little Girl. Don't put your hand near the lion's mouth."

Although I very seldom admitted it to him, Antoni꞉ always had a point—especially when it came to Peaches. Peaches had fallen out of Antoni꞉'s good graces because she failed to separate business and pleasure. Additionally, she had a blatant disregard for the rules. Antoni❖ had simply asked the girls not to fall in love with the clients, and not to have unprotected sex. Peaches had done both, and created a set of circumstances that basically ensured the demise of Antoni❖'s business.

My problem was, I saw the good parts of Peaches without balancing them with the bad. But isn't that what I had always done? Those decisions hadn't ever worked out well for me, and the situation with Peaches wouldn't be any different. I trusted Peaches. Consequently, the lion was about to eat me.

Peaches and I went on about our daily lives without a care in the world. Star's Bar and its subsidiary company were both doing very well. Since we were doing so well, Peaches introduced the idea of expanding the business. I admit, it sounded like a good idea at the time. Year two had made me more comfortable with the process, and my dealings with Angel had ensured me that he would have my back.

We could easily have expanded, but I wanted to take the time to properly vet our prospects. There were several avenues that we could have taken, but I bypassed many of them for various reasons. In some cases, they hadn't been in business long enough for me to trust their business practices. In other cases, I was able to trace them back to Antoni❖ in some way. Antoni❖ was aware that I had ventures outside of him, but I didn't want our businesses to intersect.

Admittedly, my romantic feelings for Antoni❖ had declined a little. He had been gone for two years, and I was doing my thing with Angel. Additionally, handling Antoni❖'s business made me understand that he wasn't entirely the person that I thought he was.  But I still felt obliged to carry things the right way in our business relationship. I had too much fear and respect not to do so. So I took my time, and I was meticulously sorting through our potential business clients.

Along the way, something changed with Peaches. She became less social and less accessible. There were days when she didn't answer the phone, or she was extremely short in conversation. I didn't put a lot of thought into it. Life was pulling us in a million different directions. Peaches was doing her thing, as was I. I couldn't expect that things would be the same as they were when we were "Antonio's girls". Things had changed. Life had changed us.

As far as I was concerned, all was well with the business, and that's the only responsibility that Peaches had to me. I never wanted to have her under my thumb like Antonio did. In hindsight, I understand why he had to.

The fact of the matter is, all wasn't well. That's the part where I got sloppy. On average, I was a stickler for stalking the details. I stayed on top of Antonio's books because there were other people in the picture. But Peaches and I were the only ones involved with Star's Bar. I trusted her to the point that I didn't watch her. By the time I realized my mistake, it was too late. The lion was hungry. And in not feeding her, I had basically offered myself up as a sacrificial lamb.

It was a Friday morning and I was preparing to deposit drug money, as I had many other times before. I had thrown an event a couple of weeks prior to justify why I would be making a large deposit into the sub account. After paying everything that was owed and putting up the money for the next buy, I was left with $27,000 in residual income. That was the money that would be deposited into the sub account.

Obviously, I was more organized than the average drug dealer. While I had accounts and sub accounts, most other dealers dealt strictly in cash. I stashed the cash in the business safe and left it there until I was ready to deposit.

And there it was, Friday. It was my usual deposit day. That was a routine that I had completed many times. But on that Friday, I opened the safe to find that there was no money to deposit. The safe was completely empty! I closed the safe and reopened it, as if the money would somehow reappear if I repeated the process. Unfortunately, the money was still gone.

I became dizzy, and was suddenly overcome with the urge to vomit. My bother was not just in the fact that the money was missing. Sure, that was a large part of it. But the most bothersome part of the equation was the understanding that Peaches was responsible. There were no other options to consider, as only she and I had the combination.

I loved Peaches like a sister. I had put a lot of time and energy into helping her come up, and I trusted her with my reputation and my business. I was disappointed in her, but I was also disappointed in myself. I was upset that I had failed to heed Antoni∷'s warnings. I knew I wouldn't tell him what Peaches had done. I couldn't.

I thought for a moment. Maybe there was a perfectly reasonable explanation for why the money had disappeared. I called Peaches, hoping that she'd offer an explanation that would keep her in my good graces. Of course, she didn't answer. I was disappointed, but not surprised. But yet again, I tried to give her the benefit of the doubt. Maybe she had simply stepped away from her phone. Deep down, I knew that my initial thoughts were completely on base. I just didn't want to believe them. Peaches and I wouldn't ever be the same, and I knew it.

I was tickled momentarily. When I thought back to all of the animal references that Antoni∷ had used to advise me against trusting Peaches, the comparisons seemed so varied. In some instances, he had referred to Peaches as a shrimp. In other instances, he had likened her to a lion. She was justifiably compared to both for very different reasons.

The thought of them both merged together in my mind. It was oxymoronic, yet thought provoking.

Peaches was a shrimp. She was a scavenger. She ate whatever she came across, as long as it satisfied her need at the time. But Peaches was also a lion. She was a predator with an appetite that far surpassed that of other predators.

The average lion can easily eat up to 25 pounds of food in a day's time—another fact that was given to me by Antonio. There was something incredibly dangerous about a creature that was impartial enough to eat whatever was available, and gluttonous enough to overindulge.

I imagined a creature with a lion's head and a shrimp's body. It seemed that the lion portion of the creature would eat so much that it would pop its little shrimp belly. I imagined that Peaches would pop. I imagined that all of the love, consideration, and money that I had invested would come seeping out. I too would be exuded from her little shrimp body, as Peaches had eaten me as well.

Suddenly, the shrimp with the lion's head wasn't so comical. In fact, it was quite frightening. The one thing that was set in stone was the fact that something had to be done. I sat for a moment and contemplated my next move. I knew I had pay Peaches a visit.

My phone was ringing like crazy. I hurriedly checked it each time, hoping that Peaches was calling—against all odds. But it wasn't ever Peaches, and I had no desire to answer. I drove to Peaches' apartment, hoping that she would be there and in the talking mood. Her car was there, so I knew that she was at home. Since Antonio had gotten arrested, Peaches and Cream had no other choice but to drive themselves around. I refused to pick up that part of Antonio's business.

I knocked on Peaches' door. Well, knocking is a bit of an understatement. I banged on the door, to no avail. I, again, began to experience the sensation of being nauseated. In my mind, I felt that Peaches had taken my money and skipped town. It made things official. I returned to my car, feeling completely defeated. I knew that it was over.

As I said before, I had already paid everything off—including Peaches! The money that she stole was the money that was left over. I could easily have made the money again, but Peaches and I couldn't ever be the same. That made me incredibly sad, but things were about to get worse.

Just as I was about to leave Peaches' house, I got a call from Cream. I wasn't in the mood for Cream's antics, and I considered not answering. But the thought that she may have information about Peaches' whereabouts made me work against my better judgment. I reluctantly answered the phone. "Hello?" Cream dominated the conversation immediately.

You wit' Peaches, she asked. There was a sense of urgency in her voice. It made me nervous. I told Cream that I had just left Peaches' apartment, and that I was looking for her as well. Cream paused for a moment before she addressed me. "I'm 'bout to pull up. Get ova hea Luh Gul."

If you remember, Peaches and Cream lived in the same apartment complex, but in different sections. What should have been a two minute drive, unexpectedly turned into ten. I still can't explain how I managed to drag it out for that amount of time, but I drove long enough to mull over a multitude of thoughts. Where was Peaches? What did Cream need to tell me? Why was her request for my presence so urgent? I felt completely out of control.

I arrived at Cream's apartment and found that she was standing outside waiting. She looked angry, like the mother of a disobedient child. For some reason, I felt guilty. I couldn't explain why. I hadn't committed an offense against her, but I felt that I was in trouble. I walked towards Cream, wondering what I was about to encounter. She allowed me to enter and immediately started asking questions.

"Wutchu un done Luh Gul?" That was Cream-nese for "What have you done Little Girl?" I was genuinely confused about her line of questioning. As far as I was concerned, I hadn't done anything wrong. I had started my own operation, but Antonio was aware. And while he hadn't been 100 percent on board, he gave me his blessing. He only asked that I not neglect his business for my own. I had done an amazing job of balancing the two. Well, I thought I had.

Cream started ranting in Cream-nese, and I was unable to follow the conversation. Wait, I yelled. What are you talking about? Cream paused for a moment to catch her breath. She told me to sit down and not to interrupt her. I did as I was told. I listened, and her account helped me to understand what had been happening right under my nose. Apparently, Peaches decided that my rules didn't apply to her, and it seemed that she went down the list and systematically broke them all one by one.

# Chapter 18

## ::::*Breaking All The Rules*::::

My head was spinning. Listening to Cream's account of the events both helped and terrified me. Officially, Peaches and I COULDN'T EVER be the same.

First of all, Peaches started dating Sticks behind my back. Sticks, so named for his slim build, was one of our previous "Point C" boys. He was one of the connects that I fired at Angel's request.

Per the rules, Sticks was strictly off limits—even though he didn't belong to us anymore. Yes, I broke rule number one, but that was different. Mixing business with pleasure had been beneficial to me in every way. It had been beneficial to Peaches as well. My dealings with Angel had catapulted our business to an immeasurable degree. And if I have to be honest, I was in charge. There are people who make the rules and people who have to follow them. It was obvious that our decision making processes were completely different. THAT'S what made it ok for me and not ok for Peaches. She didn't know how to properly break the rules.

Not only did Peaches break the rules, but she also moved down the food chain. I couldn't understand why she chose to get involved with someone who was beneath her. The goal was to be in the good graces of the point A people, as they were the ones with the "status". Peaches risked it all for someone who couldn't even help her advance. Sticks was a dope boy—no more, no less. Making matters worse, he always looked a little dirty. I gave Peaches more credit than that. She was very well put together and a meticulous cleaner. Sticks seemed completely contrary to what I expected of her.

Second, Peaches made the decision to start her own operation without running it past me. You may not feel that she owed me that, but she certainly did! That's the way it worked! I had to go to Antoni❖ before I could "officially" start my own operation. Everyone had someone to answer to, and Peaches should have answered to me!

And not only did she start her own operation, but she used MY money to do it! I certainly believe that Peaches let Sticks talk her into it. Of all the things that Peaches had done, she hadn't ever stolen from me. But thinking about it, I should have expected that Sticks would desire retribution. I had fired him, very dismissively at that. Of course he had an axe to grind.

I wondered how the situation with Peaches and Sticks came about. I wondered if he had sought Peaches out for that intended purpose. I wondered if they had been dealing prior to me firing him. Either way, I felt that he was responsible. I knew, first hand, that the wrong man could make the right woman do whatever he wanted her to. But that's why number one was in place. That's EXACTLY why!

Peaches had been neglected by Antoni❖ for all those years. One could only assume that she could easily be swayed if the right person came along and made her feel the right way. It's only natural. Unfortunately, her desire to be loved had come at an awful time for me.

Cream didn't know if it was the first time that Peaches had stepped out, or if something had just gone wrong THAT time. She couldn't trace the situation back to the beginning. At any rate, it was obvious that Peaches and Sticks had used my money to branch out on their own. But because Angel, my point A, would OBVIOUSLY have tipped me off, Peaches decided to reach out to another point A who was not on our approved list, breaking rule three.

Also breaking rule three, Peaches decided to sell to a Point C, completely unaware that he was connected to Antoni✱. Maybe it could have worked out and she could have just replaced the money, but it was bigger than that.

It turned out that the drugs that she received were of poor quality. Upon receipt, the Point C refused to pay. Peaches was left with drugs that she couldn't sell and no funds to honor the contract that she had entered into with the Point A. The Point A denied giving her the bad drugs, and they still wanted all the money that was due to them. Making matters worse, someone in the cycle knew Antoni✱, and the rumor mill went into overdrive.

Unable to contact Peaches, the point A had gone to Cream, thinking that the three of us were still working for Antoni✱. The point A was spreading the word that Antoni✱'s operation wasn't paying up. The point C guys were saying that Antoni✱'s operation was trying to pass off an inferior product. None of them realized that Peaches' operation was completely different from mine or Antoni✱'s. It was a disaster.

Losing $27,000 would have been a point of contention between most people, and I was obviously no exception. But the news that I had received from Cream was the worst case scenario. I would rather that Peaches had just stolen the money and skipped town. I could have come back from that. But reputation was everything in the drug business. Losing said reputation could come with a vast array of consequences— not just for me, but for Antoni✱ as well.

I had the money, and I could easily have paid off Peaches' debt. But Antoni✱ was different. He wouldn't take Peaches' indiscretion lightly.

He respected the life, and he lived by the code. Peaches had put our reputations on the line, and Antonie wouldn't take that sitting down.

All I could do was try to get out ahead of it, but that wouldn't be easy. Antonie was in prison. It wasn't as if I could just call or stop by. My only hope was to visit Antonie the next day before the news got to him in some other way. That was my only option.

I told Cream not to worry, and that I would handle everything. I stood, in an attempt to leave. Cream arose and gave me a hug. She said, "Be carefuh out dea Luh Gul." She was scared. I could see it in her eyes. Seeing Cream so worried was frightening to me. Cream was always confident and self-assured. She didn't take a lot of mess. If she was worried, it was with legitimate reasoning. I left Cream's apartment with the understanding that I had to fix something that I hadn't broken. I didn't even know where to start.

I sat for a minute, trying to digest everything that I had been fed. In that moment, none of it was worth it. I wish I hadn't trusted Peaches. I wish I hadn't started my own operation. I wish I hadn't agreed to take over Antonie's business. I wish I hadn't ever met Antonie. I went down the list of regrets, but none of them compared to what was to come. Just as I was pulling out of the apartment complex, my cellphone rang. It was Cream, telling me that Antonie's club and Sharon's salon had both been burned to the ground.

# Chapter 19

## ::::Too Far Ahead::::

*I* didn't sleep a wink that night. I got a hotel room, for fear that I would be burned alive if I stayed at home. I awoke at 6:00 the next morning, prepared to face the music. I got dressed, making sure to look nice, but not too nice. I wanted to look pretty enough to appeal to any residual attraction that Antoni❣ might have had towards me, but not so good to the point that he would think I had been using his money to further my lifestyle. I was past the favor age for Antoni❣, and I knew it. I would have to connect on something deeper. Or maybe I could just beg for forgiveness.

But then, I had a thought. My only mistake was trusting Peaches. Antoni❣ was intelligent. I thought I could make him understand that. If I could get through to Antoni❣, maybe he could straighten things out with the Point A and the Point C. That didn't help Peaches, but her broken bones were on her. It was unfortunate, but I couldn't help her. That was the web that she had woven. You know what they say. When you play dumb games, you win dumb prizes. What Peaches did was dumb, and that was on her.

I went through the search area and made my way to the back of the prison. I sat at the table in the visitation area, twiddling my thumbs, and awaiting the inevitable. Finally, Antoni❣ emerged through the double doors. Even though it had only been a week since our last visit, Antoni❣ looked completely different. He wasn't different in weight or stature, just tired—worn even. Immediately, I knew that Antoni❣ was already aware of the situation. Maybe he didn't know the whole story, but he knew some variation thereof. It was all over his face.

For the first time in the three years since his incarceration, Antoni❣ failed to greet me with a kiss and a hug. He bypassed me as I stood, never making an attempt to acknowledge my request to hug him. Antoni❣ sat and got straight to business. He interlocked his fingers and placed his forearms on the table. He looked into my eyes and began to speak.

"When I was about to go away, I only asked a few things of you. In sound mind and body, you agreed. Did you not? So, why is it, that with three months left of my sentence, I have to hear that you have failed in every area? I asked you to handle my business and I asked you not to make me look stupid. Somehow, you have managed to fail at both. Please tell me something that is going to make this make sense to me Shelonda."

I sat for a moment, ensuring that his pause indicated an invitation for response. My heart was pounding. As if Antoni❣'s temperament wasn't scary enough, he called me Shelonda. Antoni❣ didn't make a habit of calling me Shelonda unless he was angry.

I explained the story start to finish, just as Cream had explained it to me. I spilled it out like hot tea, never giving Antoni❣ an opportunity to get a word In. He sat quietly throughout my entire rant. Upon the completion of my explanation, I expected that my fault would be diminished in Antoni❣'s eyes. At the very least, I expected him to say that he understood. Instead, Antoni❣ sat back in his chair and laughed.

Do you think you've told me something that I didn't already know, he asked. I was confused. So why was he so angry? Knowing that Peaches was to blame, why was Antoni❣ still so angry with me? I guess the confusion showed on my face. Of course, Antoni❣ decided to elaborate.

But he didn't just elaborate. Antoni✺ did what he always did. He used an animal reference to break it down to me.

"Let me put it to you like this. Let's say you want a dog. Of all the dogs you could have chosen, you decided on a feral dog. You choose this dog because it needed something, and you always need to be needed. You nurture this dog and you grow to love it. Everything in your spirit tells you that it loves you too. Why wouldn't it? You have been good to that dog. But there is something that you have failed to understand. A feral dog isn't a domestic dog. They play by different rules. They have different mentalities. A domestic dog will be loyal and protective of you because you have loved and nurtured it. A feral dog will be loyal to the pack because that's how he was bred. Nonetheless, you're stuck with that wild dog, with no understanding of the danger that it presents. One day, you take your dog out for a walk in the woods. In the process, you encounter a pack of wild dogs that your dog hasn't ever been exposed to. Not only will that dog not protect you, but it will join the other dogs in the eating of you. That's what wild animals do. Helping the pack eat will always take precedence over being loyal to an outsider—even one who has loved and nurtured them. Peaches is a wild dog—a rabid, wild dog. I gave you all the information you needed about her, and you still walked her into the woods. But I guess I can blame myself as well. It was I who gave you the wild dog, allowing you to love it at your own discretion. I'm sorry Shelonda. I should have given you a poodle."

I sat for a moment, digesting what Antoni✺ had fed me. He was absolutely correct. I'd heard a lot about the things that Peaches had done, some of which came directly from the horse's mouth. I admit that I was negligent in my use of her, and I was bothered by how things had played out as a result. I couldn't believe that I had pegged the situation so incorrectly. I hated that Antoni✺ was right. I hated that I had to have that conversation on Peaches' behalf. Any explanations that were given should have been on her.

I was initially remorseful. I had every intention of trying to make things right, but Antoni♂ began to patronize me. I remember how I felt when he uttered the words. They took me to a place that I couldn't come back from. "You're a good girl Shelonda, but I shouldn't have depended on you to do anything more than multiplication. You're just not built like that." I laughed and addressed him. Antoni♂ was very good about dishing out the words, but I felt that the time had arrived for him to be on the other end.

"Ok, Antoni♂. Since you like animal references so much, here's one for you. Do you know about the mating ritual between male and female praying mantises? Well, let me enlighten you. In spite of her reverent demeanor, the female praying mantis is actually a cannibalistic predator. She lures male praying mantises in with her pheromones. When a prospective mate approaches, he engages in a courtship ritual. If deemed worthy, he is allowed to hitch a ride on the much larger female's back, with the intent to impregnate her. Without provocation, the female mantis hungrily chews off her partner's head during or shortly after the sexual encounter. Some say that the female's decision is based on her knowledge that the male thrusts more violently without the attachment of his head. It is not out of hunger or anger, but the mere desire for satisfaction. The male is simply a victim of his proximity to the female. His very existence relies on the female's decision to let him live or die. You have gotten this all wrong Antoni♂. Your businesses were hanging by a thread before I came along. If not for my intervention, they would have gone down long before your incarceration. I allowed you to jump on my back because I felt that you were worthy. And now, you want to belittle and patronize me? ME Antoni♂? The one who carried YOUR burden on MY back because YOURS wasn't big enough? That's laughable Antoni♂. You're a real piece of work. I sidetracked my entire life for your benefit, and you are ungrateful in discrediting the good that I've brought to the situation. In fact, you were negligent in getting locked up and even putting me in this position. You're a little boy. What grown man goes to jail for smoking weed and leaves someone who's not "built like that" to handle his business? And now you're all puffed up because ONE thing went out of order? Now, you're acting like I haven't been carrying you on my back? Let me explain something to you Antoni❦, because you're obviously not aware of who I am. I'm not the scavenger shrimp that will eat you because you are available. I am not the clownfish that will eat what you provide for me. I am not the lion who will eat you because you have failed to feed me. I am not the feral dog that will eat you out of loyalty to someone else. I am the female praying mantis. I am carrying you, but understand that I will eat you for no reason other than my personal desire to do so. THAT'S WHO I AM! Don't you ever forget that! And make no mistake about it. You never GAVE Peaches to me. I TOOK her, just like I took everything else."

I could see the anger rising within Antoni❦, but I didn't care. I wanted him to feel the way he had made me feel. I saw that he was searching for words, and I was happy about that. Putting him in his place made me feel confident—powerful even. Antoni❦ sat up and leaned in close. He tapped his fingers on the table, a habit that I recognized as a sign of frustration. He was very calm and deliberate. "Shelonda, I'm trying with you because I love you, but you're forcing my hand." I leaned in and attempted to imitate his tone. "You can call me Star, like all the other dope boys." Antoni❦ laughed. I could tell that he was genuinely amused. He told me that he'd always had an affinity for my spunk. Antoni❦ addressed me in a way that only he could.

"I'll tell you what. Since you want to be grown, I'm gonna treat you like I would treat anybody else. At the completion of my sentence, you will be required to sign over all of my businesses as well as your bar. You will advise your Point A that he will be working with me when I'm released, and you will set up a meeting between he and I—one to which you will not be invited. But above all else, you WILL replace Sharon's salon. That's what's gonna happen Little Girl."

It was my time to laugh. What makes you think I would do that, I asked. He only said two words. "Ask Peaches." In hindsight, I know I had pushed him too far. But there was no turning back. My words were arrogant and smug, just as I had perceived his to be.

"Really Antoni? I didn't think I had to break this down to you, but I apparently gave you too much credit. I'm not Peaches and Cream. You don't scare me. I understand that you had Peaches dancing for free to pay off a debt, but you're not going to bully me like you did her. Not only are you trying to bully me, but you're threatening me? Ask Peaches? You gonna get your goons to beat me up like they did her? Let me tell you something Antoni. You've been locked up for all this time while I've been successfully running your businesses. How relevant do you really think you are? Your goons are my goons now. And Sharon's salon? I'll replace her salon IF, and ONLY if, you guys stay on my good side. Now, let's talk about my operation. It will be a cold day in purgatory before my Point A will work with you. THAT I know for sure! Don't get so far ahead of yourself that you get left behind."

I sat back, confident in the speech that I had just delivered. Antoni readjusted and delivered his response.

"I love you, and I have every reason to believe that we can work this out when I get home. But for now, you need to learn how to stay in a child's place. Go talk to Peaches when you leave here. Come back tomorrow and let me know if you have changed your mind. Don't worry about the connects. I'll handle them. I love you. See you tomorrow Star."

I told Antoni that I would see him in a week. I sometimes replay his words in my mind. "I love you. See you tomorrow Star." There was something about the way he said it. It was ominous in nature. I couldn't put my finger on it at the time. Just as he was walking away, Antoni turned and addressed me one final time.

125

"Don't forget to set up that meeting up with your Point A. It's gonna be a cold day in purgatory. Make sure your Diablo has a jacket."

# Chapter 20

## ::::Stern Warnings::::

*I* thought about my conversation with Antoni❦ for the entire 30 minute drive back. It was cute that he still professed his love for me in the midst of his personal crisis. Even more, it was obvious that he knew about me and Angel. All things considered, Antoni❦ made it obvious that he still wanted to be with me. And if I had to be honest, I wanted to be with him too.

Angel was powerful and assertive, but he wasn't Antoni❦. Angel didn't love me, and I knew it. He had a wife and a family. We were mutually beneficial, but I wouldn't ever be anything more to him than what I was at that moment. That point wasn't ever lost upon me. Antoni❦ loved me and he made sure that I knew it. He made it obvious that he intended to step back in, and I had every intention of letting him. It was settled. Angel and I would do business, but everything else would be shut down when Antoni❦ came home.

I giggled a little when I thought about how Antoni❦ and I played off of each other. I also giggled when I thought of how Antoni❦ once insisted that he wouldn't "allow" anyone else to sleep with me. Not only had he allowed it, but he basically accepted it.

I laughed at the fact that I was terrified about my meeting with Antoni❦, but it had gone better than I could ever have imagined. But all things considered, I knew it wasn't a game. In spite of how the conversation had gone, the visit restored some things that I had lost for Antoni❦. The biggest of which was respect.

I respected Antonio, but I didn't take him seriously. I had worked hard to build my business, and I had no intention of just signing it over. I certainly had no intention of pairing him with Angel. In my heart, I wondered if I was willing to give up Antonio's businesses. I had worked hard for them too.

Antonio said that he would handle the connects. As far as I was concerned, he would straighten things out with them, and I would help him start over when he was released. I would give him what was owed to him, just as he had done for me. No more, no less.

I began to think about taking over Antonio's businesses after his release. A part of me was tickled about the prospect of us switching roles. Antonio would come home from prison and I would upgrade his wardrobe and take him on dates. I was more than willing to replace Sharon's salon, but I'd make him ask—just because. I entertained the laugh, but I didn't take that idea seriously either. Antonio wouldn't ever hear of such a thing, and I knew it.

What I did take seriously was the intimidation factor. Peaches' actions showed me that she didn't fear me. That was the difference between how people dealt with me and how people dealt with Antonio. Antonio wasn't intimidating in stature, but he was stern. I could tell that he intimidated other people. Initially, he intimidated me as well. People respected me out of respect for Antonio, but not out of fear. Something about that had to change.

I decided to pay Peaches a visit, but not for the reason that Antonio suggested. I decided to pop up and issue a stern warning. If she was home, I would "tough talk" her. Knowing that she was wrong, her fear of Antonio would keep her from challenging me. If she wasn't home, I'd wreck her house and leave her a strongly worded note.

I know that sounds crazy, but it was a trick of the goons. For some reason, people return to a house in disarray and draw a correlation between what happened to their house and what could happen to their bodies. I guess it makes sense.

I arrived at Peaches' apartment complex, and noticed that her car was still in her parking spot. In spite of my perceived brashness, I wasn't REALLY confrontational. I was disappointed to have had to go the "stern warning" route. I walked to the door and knocked. Great, I thought. Either Peaches didn't want to face me or she had really skipped town. I looked under her welcome mat. As usual, her spare key was still there. Peaches was predictable in that way.

I went back to the car to put on gloves and write the note. After folding it neatly, I wrote Peaches' name on the exterior. I walked back to the door. I knocked again, giving Peaches an opportunity to open the door on her own accord—to no avail, of course. I retrieved the key from under the mat. The moment I walked in, I knew that someone had already beaten me to the punch.

Peaches' apartment was completely trashed. It looked like the work of Antoni's goons. One way to know for sure was to check for notes. The usual places were refrigerators, televisions, bedroom mirrors—anywhere where the victim would likely look upon their return.

I walked through the mess and made my way to the kitchen. There were dirty dishes in the sink, and that really stood out. Peaches was a meticulous cleaner. I blamed the goons for most of the mess, but it wasn't like Peaches to leave dishes in the sink. She usually washed them immediately after each meal. She hated dirty dishes. I left the kitchen and headed to the bathroom. Again, the space was destroyed, but there was no note.

The only place left to search was Peaches' bedroom. I already knew I'd find more destruction, but I was hoping to also find a definitive answer to whether it was our goons or one of the connects. Considering the fact that Antoni❖ had sent me there, I was placing my bet on him.

I slowly opened the door to Peaches' bedroom. Unlike the rest of the house, the bedroom was pristine, just as she would have kept it. There was no sign that anyone had been there—not even Peaches. I searched her drawers and mirrors and found no notes. Maybe it wasn't the work of the goons. I hadn't ever known them to destroy a house without leaving a note. I thought for a moment. Peaches' bathroom was the only room left.

I went into the bathroom to read the note that I knew I would find. I did find a note. I also found Peaches and Sticks in the bathtub— naked with bags over their faces. They were parallel to each other, face to face. Peaches' left arm was resting on her hip. Prominently displayed, was the left heart—one half of the friendship bracelets that she had purchased for us. I can't explain why, but I removed my glove and unlatched Peaches' bracelet. Her arm was still warm—really warm. Unable to control my bodily functions, I vomited into the toilet.

I stared at their bodies. I knew that the images would be burned into my mind forever, but I needed to see them. I needed to see Peaches while she was still warm. I needed to see her for the last time. I lifted the bag to display her face. Peaches' mouth was agape, and her pupils had rolled. I could only see the white parts of her eyes, which had broken blood vessels running throughout them.

So many thoughts flashed through my mind. Seeing her naked body made me think of her in her prime. I remembered the tales of Peaches once being the "it" girl that all the men wanted. I remembered watching her dance and being envious of her perfect body. She was so fun. She was once so full of life, and she was gone. My eyes saw it all, but my heart and mind couldn't process it. Life wouldn't ever be the same.

I retrieved the note that was taped to the mirror. I put it into my back pocket, along with the note that I had intended to leave for Peaches. I ran to my car, hoping that I hadn't been seen. Remembering nothing of the ride, I drove to my hotel in complete silence. Once inside, I locked the hotel room door and pushed the couch in front of it—as if that would stop someone who had the intention to harm me.

I collapsed onto the bed and sobbed loudly. Peaches was gone. She was really gone! I retrieved both notes from my pocket. My hands were shaking, so much so that I could barely open the envelope. I finally got it open, fully expecting a harshly worded threat to anyone who had assisted Peaches. Instead, I found that it was meant for me!

"Remember not to get so far ahead of yourself that you get left behind. I caught a falling Star and put it in my pocket--hopefully saving it for a rainy day.

Love Always,

Your Anemone

Ps, I really wish I had gotten you a poodle instead of a feral dog."

Things became even more real in that moment. Without a shadow of a doubt, I knew that Antoni: had sent the goons to Peaches. Not only that, but I also knew that he had ordered the hit and had it executed in the 30 minutes that it took for me to drive from the prison. Three thoughts crossed my mind. 1: The goons still belonged to Antoni:. 2: Antoni: could touch me at any time and wouldn't hesitate to do so. 3: I had to get some rest, as I had to visit Antoni: bright and early the next morning.

# Chapter 21

## ::::The Saga Continues::::

Antoni: did his part and fixed the situation with the connects—just as he said he would. I was required to pay back the money that Peaches owed, but no one else had to die. I continued to handle the businesses, and all talks of Peaches and Sticks went away. It was as if they never existed. Angel and I carried on. It was business as usual in every way. Angel was the only person to somewhat mention Peaches, and I could tell that he was coming from a genuine place.

Angel insisted that I pay him a visit the day after Peaches was killed. I visited Antoni:, then went over to see Angel. He asked three questions: 1: Are you ok? 2: Do you need anything? 3: Do you need to talk to someone? It's true what they say, news travels fast. Peaches hadn't been gone for a full 24 hour period, and Angel already knew the details. His questions had cued me in to that fact.

1: Angel asked if I was ok because he knew that Peaches was gone. He was aware of how close we were. 2: He asked if I needed anything because he knew that I took a loss on the money that Peaches stole. Even so, I still had to pay the money she owed. Boy, Peaches' Point A really got me. 3: He asked if I needed to talk to someone because he knew that I had found Peaches' body. He told me that he could put me in contact with some good people. I declined.

Present day, I'm aware that I should have taken him up on his offer. There was such a stigma around mental health, but I needed counseling more than anyone I knew. Angel and I talked openly about my future. I informed him of Antoni:'s request, to which he only stated "I'll see him." He never asked my position on the matter. He simply said "I'll see him."

I continued to visit Antonio, and I kept him abreast with all pertinent information. I tried to pretend that everything was the same, but it wasn't. How could it be? There were so many elephants in the room. We didn't talk about things. We pretended to be unaffected, but we weren't. I wasn't ok, and I don't think that Antonio was either. He loved Peaches too. I can't imagine that he felt ok about what he had done. Yet, life just continued to move.

Antonio was set to come home three months after "Operation Peaches." Per our agreement, I went to the prison to get him on the day that he was to be released. I addressed the receptionist and sat down to await Antonio's exit. Twenty minutes into the wait, the receptionist called me up to the desk. She told me that Antonio had already been released. What, I exclaimed. Released? I had talked to Antonio two days prior, and it was always the plan for me to pick him up. I left feeling confused and dejected.

There was a lot to the story of Shelonda and Antonio. But for some reason, his decision to leave with someone else was the ultimate betrayal. I think it was the rejection. The fact that Antonio had rejected me was jarring to me. It would have been fine if I didn't want him. But him not wanting me created an issue. Had my anemone found another clownfish? In my heart, I knew that had to be so. I hated the feeling of rejection, and that always caused me to want the other person more. I can't explain it.

I thought back to how bothered I was when Brandon broke up with me for Toya Boone. I remembered how hurt I was when Ron started giving Mom attention instead of me. I thought back to how angry I was when I found out about KEN and Melonie. On each of those occasions, I wanted the person even more after I had been hurt.

I wish I'd had a better understanding of myself. I wish I had realized that I was enough without having to be wanted by someone who didn't really have the best of intentions. That would have made life so much easier. Maybe that would have changed everything. I wish.

I made the drive, wondering where I stood with Antoni. After running a few errands, I finally made my way home. Living up to his ability to surprise me, Antoni was already there. He was quietly sitting on my couch, awaiting my arrival—just as he had been on the night that I found out that he was going to prison. Antoni had parked in the rear to conceal his presence.

Well, I said. "Look what the cat drug in." Antoni stood and extended his arms to hug me. I watched him, shocked and amazed that he had shown up like it was just a regular day. I bypassed him and sat on the opposite end of the couch. So, I said. "I see you found a ride." Come here, said Antoni. I laughed. I told him that if he wanted to be near me, he would have waited for me to pick him up. A little more stern, Antoni told me to come to him. I pivoted my body towards him, still sitting on the couch. I stared at him, waiting to see if he would come to me. I wanted to know if he thought I was worth it.

Antoni walked over to where I was seated on the couch. He sat beside me and interlocked his fingers with mine. Antoni looked directly into my eyes as he spoke. "You know I love you right? You just have to learn that I'm not on your time." I didn't speak. He told me that I wasn't cut out for that life, and he was sorry to have brought me into it. Antoni apologized for the "Peaches situation", as if he had simply stepped on her foot. He admitted that things had gone too far, and he wanted to know if we could start over.

Start over, I asked. "How do we just start over after everything that we have been through?" Just bow out Little Girl. That was his answer. Just bow out, as if that would fix everything. Just bow out, as if that would absolve me of the guilt related Peaches' death and Sharon losing her salon. Apparently, the simple act of bowing out would change the past and allow us to start over. For the first time, Antonio's solution didn't impress me.

Antonio told me that he wanted me to let him be the man. He asked me to let him run the businesses and he would take care of me. "We can make this easy. We can just start over." I thought for a moment. As much as I wanted to keep up the façade, I knew he was right. I was tired. More than being tired, I was scared.

Truthfully, I knew I could resist. Legally, Antonio didn't have a leg to stand on. We hadn't made provisions for him to retrieve his businesses upon his return. But the goons didn't play by legal rules. By their standards, I knew that any day could be the day that I regretted being resistant. I didn't want to end up in my bathtub.

Antonio cupped my chin in his hands. "What are we gonna do? Are we gonna make this easy?" I told him that I'd give him everything he asked for. Antonio looked into my eyes and addressed me. "That's a good girl. And this Diablo thing? That's over, right?" I nodded my head, acknowledging that I would end my relationship with Angel. Antonio kissed me. And even though he had swindled me out of my business, I gave in. Even though I knew he'd had Peaches killed, I gave in. Even though I knew I was always within 30 minutes of being next, I gave in.

I arranged a meeting between Angel and Antonio. True to his word, Antonio did not allow me to attend. When it was all said and done, Angel and Antonio exited the office together and joined me in the lobby. Angel shook my hand and addressed me. "It was wonderful working with you Star." He then turned and addressed Antonio. "I look forward to working with you." He walked away without saying another word. I guess the cold day in purgatory had arrived. Just like that, Angel and I were over. Just like that, the story of Shelonda and Antoni: continued. And just like that, Star fell out of the sky.

In letting go of Star, I thought about my connection to Peaches. She was my partner. She was a large part of Star being able to rise. I thought about her all the time, but I didn't openly grieve her. I couldn't. She just went away, taking with her our memories and our special bond.

Peaches had crossed me and caused a lot of trouble for a lot of people. Even with the loss of $27,000, I would have let it slide a thousand times over to erase the mental image of her and Sticks in that bathtub. I thought about it every time I closed my eyes. Even worse, I knew that I had played a part in it. I found it extraordinarily difficult to forgive myself. Even harder, was forgiving Antoni:.

I thought back to the creature with the head of a lion and the body of a shrimp. Peaches had succumbed to the nature of the beast. The shrimp in her ate with indifference. The lion in her overindulged. And in the end, she popped. Peaches just popped. And with all the hurt in my heart and the anger in my spirit, I had to continue as if Antoni: and I were just starting over. We just kept moving.

In thinking about it, I now realize something profound. For as hurt as I was over losing Peaches, my desire to rectify her death was overshadowed by my desire to be with someone. I didn't want to be lonely. I stayed with Antoni: because I didn't want to be lonely.

Antoni: didn't rush to change the legalities of the situation. He knew I would cooperate. I certainly had no desire to fight him. It was a month into Antoni:'s release before we returned to the lawyer's office to sign the papers—at my insistence. By that point, I just needed it to be over. I needed to be free.

Antoni: and I went his lawyer's office. I found myself looking at the sign, just as I had when Antoni: had signed his businesses over to me. The Law Office of David L Herkowitz Esq. Things had certainly changed since we had visited last. Three years prior, I was a scared young girl with a large undertaking ahead of me. On that day, I was a boss. I was saddened by some of the events that had taken place, but proud of what I had been able to accomplish. I felt that I could let go, knowing that I hadn't lost anything—other than Peaches.

I gave Antoni all of his businesses back, in addition to Star's Bar. I didn't even want it anymore. He promised to keep the name the same, as a sign of the respect that he had for me and my hard work. By that point, I didn't care much about his respect either. I only asked Antoni not to become involved with the Point C girls that I handed over to him. I didn't want them to feel that they had anything over me. Yep, that's where my mind was.

Antoni gladly accepted everything back. He did, however, keep me as the beneficiary of his life insurance. Of course he made a joke out of the situation. He told me that he didn't trust me to run his businesses. But due to the fact that I loved to give orders, he trusted me with his funeral arrangements. We both laughed. Even in the tensest of situations, Antoni and I could usually find an avenue for humor. I loved that. Maybe we really could just start over.

I reclaimed my spot on top of the hierarchy. Only there was no hierarchy. Peaches was dead. And since the strip club was no longer, Cream had basically evaporated. I hadn't heard anything from Sharon, and I had no desire to face her. Her salon was her passion, and I knew that. It was hard for me to think about seeing her, knowing that I had inadvertently contributed to its demise. I had crossed Sharon by dealing with Antoni, but I still loved and respected her. She was the first person to respect me and demand that I respect myself. I carried that guilt every day until it was replaced with a new guilt—a guilt that would surpass every other guilt in my life.

I was surprised by how easily I fell back into my role. I thought that I would feel more slighted about falling back. Antoni﹖ did exactly what he said he would do. He took over Star's Bar and kept the name the same. He kept the system of accounts and sub accounts, and I kept the books. And even though he knew that I had my own money, Antoni﹖ continued to provide for me. I allowed him to present the image of being the man. We both pretended that things were the same as they were before he went away.

But so much had changed otherwise. Things felt different without the strip club. I missed the girls, and I missed Cream and Peaches. Although our basic situation was the same, things felt completely different between me and Antoni﹖. We joked around a lot. That's who we were. But Antoni﹖ no longer smiled at me the same way. He didn't look lovingly into my eyes anymore. He called me Little Girl in passing, but it wasn't the same. It didn't have the cute affection attached to it. Everything felt so strange.

Antoni﹖ and I no longer had great sex. When we did have sex, it wasn't our usual passionate sex. It was "means to an end" sex. It was quick and to the point, which was unfortunate.

Sex with Antoni﹖ was amazing before, but that definitely wasn't related to his "girth". Antoni﹖ was a caring and sensual lover. He was skilled in the art of touch. He was quite good in the oral department as well. But being perfectly honest, Antoni﹖ was small—down there. He was quite small. The penis size wasn't an issue when he compensated otherwise. But cutting the sensual part out of the equation was problematic, to say the least.

I started to understand why Cream had stopped caring about having sex with Antoni﹖. If that was what she was getting, I could see why she hadn't cared to have it at all. It was the type of penis that could only be enjoyed with feelings involved. Otherwise, it was pretty awful.

I began to think of myself as the new Cream. I started to care a little less, and Antoni☙ was starting to feel more like a source of income than a boyfriend. I suspected that there was someone else, someone newer and younger. That was Antoni☙'s pattern of behavior. I wondered if it was one of the Point C girls, and that thought infuriated me. Yet, the Antoni☙ and Shelonda show remained for another year. With the regret, anger, sadness, ill feelings, awful sex, and suspicions, the saga still continued....

# Chapter 22

## ::::All Good Things::::

*T*hey say that all good things come to an end. In our case, a stale and mediocre situation was about to come to an end. There are instances where endings are necessary. I can admit that my relationship with Antoni: had started to get to that point. But the way our situation ended would haunt me for years to come. Actually, I think it may haunt me forever.

It was 2005 and I was 25 years old. Antoni: was 37. I spent the day getting prepared, as Antoni: and I were leaving for Hawaii the next day. I was surprised that Antoni: had suggested the trip. It seemed that he and I were more like business partners than people in a relationship. We handled business and settled into a comfortable routine. But that's all it was—comfort. I no longer had those warm, fuzzy feelings. I didn't think that Antoni: did either. We just existed, with very little care and no direction. Things had certainly gone downhill.

But a week before that day, something changed. Suddenly, Antoni: wanted to be around me all the time. It wasn't exactly like it used to be, but I saw glimpses of the old Antoni: flickering through our dysfunction. He smiled at me again. He looked into my eyes. He touched me when he spoke to me. He flirted with me and called me Little Girl. I felt that old thing trying to come through.

Unexpectedly, Antoni: told me that we needed a break from the businesses. He suggested a trip to Hawaii, and I was all for it. Although we kept up the front for outside purposes, I knew that Antoni: and I were on our last leg. And if I had to be honest, I missed him. I saw him every day, but I missed him. I missed us.

I was hoping that the trip would bring us a little closer to where we used to be. Hawaii was where we went on our first big vacation together. It was the trip that solidified my place in Antoni•'s value system. It held a special meaning for me, and I felt that it held a special meaning for Antoni• as well.

I prepared myself for our trip. I arose early and got my hair braided—at Antoni•'s request, of course. The African women, whom I had come to know well, braided my hair beautifully. Afterwards, I went to the nail salon, where I got a French manicure and the best pedicure that I'd had in a while—also at Antoni•'s request. Antoni• was very particular. And while I usually chose things that were contrary to what he would have chosen, I obliged that day. I told him that he could have things his way, as thanks for the vacation.

Antoni• and I ate lunch together. We went to the same seafood restaurant where we had gone on our first date. Unlike the first time, the restaurant was full and buzzing with the sounds of laughter. Also unlike the first date, I was skilled in the art of eating lobster. I thought about our first time there and how far we had come since then. It was such a happy day. It was a beautiful spring day—not too hot, not too cold. We ate outside and enjoyed the sunshine. It was hard to imagine that anything bad could happen on a day like that. But isn't that how I felt the first time that Ron took me to the shack?

We drove to Antoni•'s office. While I was reviewing his paperwork, Antoni• came in and locked the door. I knew exactly what that meant. We both smiled at the prospect of having quiet office sex. Antoni• walked over to my side of the desk. He picked me up and sat me on his desk. Just as he had done on that first day, Antoni• undressed me. He looked into my eyes as we had the best sex that we'd had that entire year. It was sensual. It was erotic. It was amazing. Antoni❖ and I laughed when we were done, reflecting on how he had to cover my mouth to muffle the moans. It was incredible!

Antoni❖ took me to my car, and we parted company. There was nothing special about our goodbye. It was a simple peck on the lips and a promise to meet up later. It wasn't special, but it was normal. It was comfortable. It was perfect. The day was reminiscent of old times—back before things were complicated by hurt and betrayal.

I went my way, and Antoni❖ went his. I collected some last minute items and made my way home. In spite of the fact that Antoni❖ and I were set to leave at 8:00 the next morning, I still hadn't finished packing. I looked at the clock. It was 7:30, and I promised Antoni❖ that I would be there by 9:00. I knew that I was going to be late. I was notorious for being late, and Antoni❖ hated it. I showered and got dressed. It was 9:42, and I was just leaving to make the drive to Antoni❖'s. He'd be annoyed, but he would be ok. We were leaving for paradise in the morning. How could he stay mad with me?

I made the drive to Antoni❖'s. I parked in the back, just as I did every other time I'd visited. I retrieved my overnight bag from the front seat, leaving my luggage in the trunk. I knocked on the door. Antoni❖ greeted me with a smile. "You're late Little Girl." He cupped my chin and gave me a peck on the lips. I ordered Chinese, he said.

Antoni❖ took my bag with one hand and used the other to escort me into the house. He dropped me off in the living room and took my bag to his bedroom. Antoni❖ returned to the living room and took his place on the couch. Come here Little Girl, he said. I walked over and straddled his body. I asked him if he liked little girls. We both laughed. It was reminiscent of the first time he kissed me in his office.

I draped my arms around Antoni♥'s neck, and he placed his hands on my butt. We kissed. It was a passionate kiss. He ran his fingers through my braids, just as he used to. As crazy as it sounds, everything came right back. The love, the attraction, the butterflies, all of it. I realized why I had fallen for him in the first place. That entire day had shown me why. He was amazing. He was sooooo amazing!

Antoni♥ reached over and retrieved his cell phone from the end table. He smiled while entering something. It was the smile that he gave when he was about to do something nice for me. Antoni♥ pressed play and placed his phone back on the table. A song started playing. It was "Where Do Broken Hearts Go?" by Whitney Houston.

Antoni♥ asked me to stand. I did as he requested. He smiled as he addressed me. "Dance with me Little Girl." We danced and kissed. Antoni♥ sang the lyrics to the song. It was one of the most wonderful moments that I have ever experienced, past or present.

> ♪ "Where do broken hearts go
> Can they find their way home
> Back to the open arms
> Of a love that's waiting there
> And if somebody loves you
> Won't they always love you
> I look in your eyes
> And I know that you still care for me" ♪

That was the moment when it all started to make sense. Everything that had transpired over the course of that week had been Antoni♥'s attempt to get us back to where we used to be. The words of that song hadn't ever resonated so deeply with me. Antoni♥ wanted to find his way back "home". And the fact that we really loved each other guaranteed that we would always love each other. Antoni♥ held me tightly—like he didn't want to let me go. I didn't want him to let me go.

The doorbell rang and Antoni❣ went to retrieve our food. He passed me an eggroll. I opened my container and already knew that I would find my favorite—General Tso chicken with extra sauce, lo mein with no onions, and extra broccoli. I looked up to smile at Antoni❣. He was already smiling. I absolutely loved his smile. We talked about an assortment of things over dinner. We laughed. The conversation was easy and effortless, just as it was before. That's why I loved him. That's the Antoni❣ I had fallen in love with.

Antoni❣ looked at the clock before addressing me. "It's after 11:00 Little Girl. Let's go to bed." I asked if we were going to bed or if we were going to sleep. Again, we both laughed. He said "I love you Little Girl. I'm never gonna love anybody the way I love you." I told him that I loved him as well. Antoni❣ picked me up and walked me into his bedroom. I loved when he did that.

Just then, the doorbell rang. Antoni❣ and I exchanged glances. I could tell that he was genuinely confused about who would be visiting at that time of night. Antoni❣ told me to stay in the bedroom. He said that he would get rid of whoever was at the door. I did as he requested. Besides, I wanted to change into my lingerie before he came back into the bedroom. I changed clothes and seductively positioned myself on the bed. I was there for approximately ten minutes before I started to get impatient. We had a busy morning ahead, and hopefully a busy night. I needed Antoni❣ to come to bed.

I decided to investigate the cause of Antoni❣'s delay. I grabbed my robe and walked towards the door. I heard voices. It sounded as if Antoni❣ was arguing with someone. I should have stayed in the bedroom. I should have done what I was told. If I had the wits of a normal person, I would have. But my curiosity got the better of me.

I often wonder if things would have transpired differently if I hadn't come out of the bedroom. Even more, I've wished a million times that I had stayed home that night. I've also wondered if I was just meant to be there—like a greater power knew that I would need to have the good memories that we created that day. Or maybe it was karma. In either case, I can't take back what happened, as much as I wish I could. All good things come to an end.

I tied my robe and walked out of the bedroom. As I got closer to the voices, a sinking feeling came over me. I knew something was wrong. I entered the living room to see two familiar faces. I locked eyes with Antoni� first. There was something in his expression that made me feel panicked. He looked sad, maybe even scared. My eyes quickly made their way to the right, where I saw the second familiar face. She was angry and crying. She was my karma. She was Sharon.

# Chapter 23

## :::: The End ::::

$M$y mind couldn't grasp an adequate assessment of the situation. I could have cut the tension with a knife. Both Sharon and Antoni❣ stopped talking when I entered the room. Sharon turned to face me and started to laugh through her tears. It wasn't the laugh when something is actually funny. It was the universal sign of disbelief.

UNBELIEVABLE, Sharon screamed. I'm so sorry, I said. I tried to explain, but Sharon continued to laugh in the same sarcastic manner. She was shaking. It was incredibly scary. I hadn't ever seen that expression on her face, or anyone else's face for that matter. I continued to apologize. "Sharon, I'm so sorry. We never meant for this to happen."

Sharon looked at Antoni❣, and then quickly turned her attention back to me. Oh yeah, she said. "You're dumber than I thought." Sharon looked back at Antoni❣ and smiled as she addressed him. "Bae, do you want to tell her, or do you want me to?" I looked at Antoni❣. He had tears in his eyes. Don't do this Sharon, he said. "Just leave. We can talk about this later." I addressed him. "Antoni❣, what is she talking about?" He didn't answer.

Maybe you should have a seat, said Sharon. I told her that I'd prefer to stand. More forceful the second time, Sharon told me to sit down. I did as I was told. I needed to hear whatever she was about to say as badly as she needed to say it.

Antoni❣ was positioned to my left, Sharon to my right. Antoni❣ didn't offer any more resistance, fully aware that he couldn't catch the bomb that Sharon was about to drop. We both allowed her to speak uninterrupted. The words that she uttered changed everything that I thought I knew. Sharon turned to me and began to speak.

"Let me start from the beginning Londa. And trust me when I tell you that the beginning began long before you could ever have imagined. You say that you and Antoni⁑ were never meant to happen? That's the biggest joke of the day. Maybe YOU thought it wasn't supposed to happen this way, but much of this was planned long ago. Everything started when your mom kicked you out of the house. As usual, you were needy, just as you always are. I saw that as my opportunity, and I moved. I took you in with a plan in mind. The flaw in the plan came when you decided to move out and move in with KEN. I tried to talk you out of it, but you HAD to go. You would have done anything for the love of a man. I guess some things never change. But as luck would have it, KEN got locked up. Once again, you were needy. And once again, I saw my chance. Understand that the situation between you and Antoni⁑ never got past me. In fact, I sent him to you. Do you remember when your car broke down in 1998? I was NEVER too tired to pick you up. Do you really think I would trust you around my man after you willingly slept with your mom's husband and got pregnant? I sent him to you for a very specific reason. Why? Because I was you before you were you. I was Antoni⁑'s accountant, legal counsel, business partner, and confidant. The same way you worked the books is the same way that I worked the girls. Yeah, that's right. Antoni⁑ and I set you up to get worked. The plan was for him to reel you in and get you to either strip in the club or get into the escort business—either of which would have been lucrative for us. That's what it was supposed to be. That was what you were worth to him. But things started going into a different direction. Every time I asked about the status of the operation, Antoni⁑ would tell me that he was working on it. I knew something was wrong. I sensed the change. Suddenly, he was spending more time with you, buying you more, and taking you places. I knew the signs. I had phased Cream out that exact same way. I took a step back to see how Antonio was going to handle things. Of course he disappointed me, because that's what he does. I asked him to choose, and he refused. All the while, he was insisting that I remain loyal to him. I felt stupid. I was loyal to a man who basically told me that he did not have the ability to be faithful to anyone. So, I did what I had to do. I called his probation officer to tell her that Antonio was smoking marijuana and it was assured that he would not be able to pass a drug test. When nothing happened, I called a supervisor. I'm to assume that you both still think that his regular officer just went away. Maybe that was messed up, but it was worth it to me. If I wasn't going to be happy with him, you certainly weren't either. As a bonus, I could reclaim the businesses while he was gone. That would have worked out just fine. But unbeknownst to me, Antonio had signed all of the businesses over to you! YOU! Do you know how angry and humiliated I was? Do you know how it felt to watch you take my place? It was bad enough watching Antonio water my seeds. But you? You didn't deserve to be there. You didn't deserve to benefit from what I had worked hard for. Making matters worse, my salon got burned down because you and Peaches were too stupid to run a business that was fully functioning when it was handed over to you. Yet, Antonio forgave you. Meanwhile, I had to watch you still handle the businesses and live the life, while I did hair out of my basement. That just wasn't fair. I talked to Antonio, and we agreed to work things out. I picked him up from the prison when he was released. I dropped him off, with the expectation that he was going to end things with you. He promised that he would, and I believed him. Everything was fine. He was putting in his time, and he promised to purchase another salon for me. It was stupid, but I believed him. But over the course of the last week or so, something changed. Antonio was distant, cold even. I knew the signs. I knew there was someone else. I know that man! This morning, I woke up in the same bed that you were about to sleep in. I made that man breakfast. That man told me that he loved me and sent me on my way. Not two hours later, that man called me and told me that he couldn't be with me anymore. He didn't talk to me face to face. He didn't offer any explanations. He just told me that he was letting me go, as if I were an employee. That's all I meant to him. I came here tonight to do one of two things. I wanted to either fix what was broken or finally find a way to let go. If I had come here tonight and found out that Antoni❣ just didn't want me, I could have handled that. I made up my mind that I would let go if that's what he really wanted. I came here for closure either way. I deserve that. But instead of closure, I found you. YOU! The person who I gave a place to stay! The person who I allowed to work at my salon, even though you neglected the responsibility over and over again! The person who I provided transportation for, at the expense of my own convenience! The person who took everything that should have been mine! And now, you both want me to just leave, like I didn't give you both everything that you've ever wanted and needed—including each other! Just leave? I don't think so."

I looked at Antoni❣. He and I were both crying. He looked incredibly sad. But in a split second, the sadness in his eyes turned into horror. What are you doing, he screamed. My eyes traveled to the right. There Sharon stood, her face saturated with tears. My eyes traveled down and saw that she was holding a gun.

The whole event played out in slow motion. It was like a theatrical event. Antoni❣ and I both begged Sharon to put the gun down. In the coldest, most inauspicious tone, Sharon said "You've taken everything away from me Antoni❣. Now, I'm going to take everything away from you."

It all happened so quickly, yet so slowly. There was nothing I could do to change Sharon's mind. She wanted me dead, and a small part of me didn't blame her. I closed my eyes to prepare for the inevitable. I vividly recall every single second.

I heard Antoni☂ screaming. "Noooooooo!" I heard the sound of the bullet leaving the chamber. I smelled the smoke. I felt the heavy sensation of something hitting my chest. I smelled the blood. I tasted it in my mouth. I felt it on my skin.

I opened my eyes and saw the shock and sadness on Sharon's face. I heard her voice. I've replayed it in my mind so many times. She was crying and screaming. "What did I do? What did I do?" Sharon placed the gun against her right temple. She uttered three words "You did this." She pulled the trigger.

Sharon's body fell to the floor. I watched helplessly as each individual fragment of her skull separated from the one adjacent. I turned my head to the left, searching for Antoni☂. He wasn't there. I looked down and saw that he was resting on my chest. Bloodied and motionless, his body slid onto the floor—a bullet hole prominently displayed between his eyes.

It was in that moment that I realized something. Intentionally or unintentionally, Antoni☂ had taken that bullet for me. I jumped into action. I started searching his pockets for his cell phone. I hoped that against the odds, he could be saved. Antoni☂ was wearing gray sweatpants. They were saturated with his blood. I searched his left pocket, to no avail. I slid my hand into his right pocket. There was no cell phone. There was, however, a beautiful platinum, princess cut engagement ring. My engagement ring. ▫

# Chapter 24

## ⸺Smile⸺

$B$oth Sharon and Antonio passed away that night. I handled the details and put them both away nicely. Many may wonder why I handled their arrangements. The answer is simple. I felt obliged. All things considered, both Sharon and Antonio had been good to me in so many ways. They both had selfish motives, but I couldn't ignore the contributions that they had made to my life.

Taking her motives out of the equation, I owed a lot to Sharon. Not only did I owe her, but I still had a love for her that many people won't understand. She was tied to so many parts of my life.

Sharon was tied to the first time that I actually felt pretty. I was forced to remember the first time that she did my hair. I experienced a feeling that I hadn't ever felt before. She gave me the support that I needed to present myself in a confident manner.

Additionally, Sharon was the first person to speak to me without judgment. She listened to me. She never made me feel insignificant about my thoughts and feelings. Sharon was the first person who told me to respect myself. She told me to demand respect from those around me. She was my first example of a confident, dark skinned woman. She made me feel that I should be that as well. I couldn't forget that.

I often wondered when things had changed. Nothing in me felt that she wasn't a true friend in the beginning. I honestly felt that she loved me. So, what changed?......Antonio. That's what changed. I can't pinpoint the time, but I believe I have figured it out.

I was around a lot in the beginning. I'd like to believe that Sharon had a genuine affection for me. If I had to guess, I'd say that it was Antonio who planted the seed. That doesn't absolve Sharon of the part that she played, as Antonio would not have been able to start the plan without her, but it was bigger than that. I understood it.

Very few people will understand the force that Antonio was. You'd have to experience it. He was ruthless and predatory in most cases. But if he loved you, there wasn't anything that he wouldn't do for you. He could make you feel that there wasn't anything that you shouldn't do for him. That's the power that he held.

Antonio could make you feel as if you were the only person who existed. He was loving and attentive in a way that made you understand how he felt about you. You didn't have to ask. You just knew. The look in his eyes told you. The softness of his touch told you. The way he held your hand, cupped your chin, or kissed your forehead. Everything he did made you understand how he felt about you.

Antonio was the first man to make me feel wanted. He encouraged me to speak my mind, even when he was the target of my cross words. He allowed me to be free. I never knew what would anger KEN, but I always knew the end result. But Antonio was so easy going. At most, he'd smirk and say "Ok now Little Girl." But he never raised his voice to me. He was the only man who never made me feel afraid. It was magical. HE WAS MAGICAL!

I had been on both sides of Antonio's favor, and that's why I understood. When you were good with Antonio, you'd do anything to keep that feeling. When you weren't good, you'd do anything to get it back. It was like a magnetic pull. No amount of pushing would suffice. He could pull you back at his will. I hadn't ever experienced that. It was a once in a lifetime feeling that far surpassed any love that I'd experienced before or after him—even present day. I didn't just want Antonio, I needed him. Not financially. I needed his aura, his presence, his energy. His soul was connected to mine. His soul is still connected to mine.

How can you experience that and not fight for it? I understood why Sharon's need for Antonio had caused her to betray me. It was the same need that caused me to betray her. It made her betray Cream. It made Cream betray Peaches. Even knowing everything, I would have betrayed anyone if I could have had him back, even for a short amount of time. How could I really be upset with Sharon?

A month after the funerals, I was contacted by Antonio's lawyer. He said that it was urgent that we meet. I made the trip to his office, never knowing why I was there. I parked in a space in the very front and exited my car—the beautiful Jaguar that Antonio had purchased for me. I read the sign. "The Law Office of David L Herkowitz Esq". I thought about being there on two other occasions. The first was when Antonio signed his businesses over to me before he went to prison. The second was when I had to give them all back—along with my bar.

An extremely heavy feeling came over me. Regardless of the circumstances, I would have given anything to have those days back. I would rather have been anywhere with Antonio than to suffer the hurt of being without him. I pushed the tears away and went into the office. I didn't have time for a breakdown.

 Mr. Herkowitz greeted me and shook my hand. He proceeded to tell me that Antonio had left some things for me. I was surprised. He told me that Antonio's businesses had been distributed to his surviving relatives, as he didn't have a living will and testament. He did, however, leave a hand-written letter for me.

"My sweet Little Girl,

I want you to know that I love you more than life itself. I won't ever love anyone the way that I love you. If you are reading this, I can no longer fulfill my promise to take care of you forever. I won't burden you with my business, as we both know how that ended the last time. I did, however, leave a little something for you. I know that you can do this thing without me. Go to school. Do what you should have done—what I should have pushed you to do from the beginning. I'm taking the Star out of my pocket. Shine Little Girl.

Love Always,

Your Anemone"

In spite of my best efforts, I broke. There was nothing I could do to stop the tears from flowing. After everything that we had been through, none of that mattered. Antonio's death left a gaping hole in my spirit that couldn't be fixed with the largest of patches. Antonio was gone, taking my soul with him. Yet, I was still alive—a shell of a person with no soul. In that moment, I wished that Sharon had killed me too. Not brave enough to end my life, I had to go on.

I had to go on, and I had to face the truth. Every single thing that had happened was my fault. It was all on me. If I had turned Antonio away when he arrived that first time, he and I wouldn't ever have been. If I hadn't raced Sharon for Antonio, I wouldn't ever have taken her place. If I hadn't held my relationship with Antonio so closely, I would have taken Cassidy from Mom. If I hadn't ever started my own drug operation, Peaches wouldn't ever have stolen from me. If I hadn't started my own operation, neither Sharon's salon nor Antonio's club would have been burned to the ground—making it harder for Sharon and Cream to make a living. If I hadn't verbally annihilated Antonio at the prison, I wouldn't have felt responsible for Peaches' death. If I hadn't stayed with Antonio, it would have been easier for him to make it work with Sharon. If he had made it work with Sharon, they would both still be alive. It was my fault. It was all my fault.

Inevitably, I had to arrive at a conclusion. In getting so far ahead of myself, I, and everyone that I held dear had gotten left behind. I failed myself, Antonio, Sharon, Cream, Peaches, and Cassidy. How could anyone live with that guilt? In being the person that I was, it was impossible for me to have ever properly nurtured any friendship or relationship. It wasn't the nature of who I was at the time. I vowed to change things in the future. It wasn't until that moment that I realized how important relationships were. I went through everything alone, and I never wanted to experience that feeling again.

Antonio left me 1.5 million dollars. He also left me an insurance policy that far surpassed what I had paid for his and Sharon's funerals. I knew that it would be difficult, but I decided that I needed to live my life in a way that would make Antonio proud. I had to. I sobbed throughout the entire visit with the lawyer. I needed to. I needed to release.

I left the lawyer's office and went to a coffee shop down the street. If at no other point in time, that was the perfect day for sugar and caffeine. I approached the barista. "I'll take a cinnamon roll and a large coffee. Lots of sugar and cream, please." I heard a voice behind me. "I'll have the same." I turned and displayed a stiff smile—the type you give when you want to acknowledge someone's presence without giving them too much attention. It was, however, the first time that I'd smiled that day.

He walked up to the barista and told her to add my order to his. I told him that his generosity wasn't necessary. You smiled, he said. "You should do that more often." The man retrieved the tray containing both of our orders. He walked towards a table. Instinctively, I followed him.

The man and I sat and talked. I laughed for the first time since the day that Sharon killed Antonio. He made me feel relaxed, like some of the weight was being lifted. Is there any way I can take you on a proper date, he asked. Sure, I said. Again, I smiled.

He and I exchanged numbers, and he agreed to call to see when I was free. I immediately knew that he was different than any man with whom I had previously been associated. I didn't know, however, that he would become my next KEN.

# Excerpt From Book Three—THE END

## My Guy

*I* got dressed and looked at myself in the mirror. I looked good. I looked sophisticated. I was wearing a form fitting, black dress with black pumps. My hair was pulled back and pinned on both sides. I had spent a considerable amount of time creating a beautiful wave pattern in my hair, which fell mid-back. It was beautiful. I was beautiful.

I looked over an assortment of jewelry. That was the part I hated the most—finding a balance. It was hard for me to find the middle ground between just enough and not too much. I chose a simple pair of diamond earrings and a diamond tennis bracelet. Yes, that was just enough. I decided to finish the look with a simple, black clutch that had a single diamond as a button. I applied some blush to my cheeks and a pale pink lip gloss. Everything fell just as it should have. I looked perfect.

I took one last look before getting into my car and driving downtown. For the most part, it was my preference to have my dates pick me up and take me home. I just felt like that was what a man was supposed to do. But these were different circumstances. I had a vested interest in deviating from the norm. Every aspect of that situation was atypical.

I parked and took one last look in the mirror. Again, I looked perfect. I walked into the restaurant, making sure to look secure and confident. May I help you, asked the hostess. She asked if she could help me, but she looked as if she wanted to do anything but. She looked at me like I didn't belong there, as if I were inferior.

I told her that I had a 7:00 reservation. She smiled stiffly and said, "Oh you do?" I didn't like her tone or her arrogance. I removed my Dolce and Gabana sunglasses. I had paid $1250 for them. I looked into the hostess' eyes and spoke.

"Listen Sweetheart, I can only assume that your procrastination is a habit of the poor, as people of my status understand that time is money. Now, would you like to lead me to my table, or do I need to tell your manager how much you like to waste time?"

She looked embarrassed. But most of all, she looked defeated. That was enough for me. She asked me who I was there to meet. I responded in the most condescending manner I could muster. "My date is the richest man here." The hostess looked confused. But, instead of engaging in verbal combat, she said "Yes. Right this way ma'am." I returned my glasses to their original position. I wanted to present that same confidence when I reached the table.

And there he was, my new guy. He stood and greeted me with a kiss on the cheek. The hostess attempted to walk away, but he stopped her. Excuse me, he said. She turned around. She looked as though she felt inconvenienced, but she dared not say so.

He turned and addressed me. "Is there anything you require Sweetheart?" I looked at the hostess, who wanted to be anywhere but there. Yes, I said. "As a matter of fact, can you bring me a Whipped Dorda please?" He interjected. "Isn't that the delectable chocolate drink with the whipped cream on top?" It most certainly is, I said. We both paused, then laughed. The hostess shook her head to signal that she was clear on everything, both stated and otherwise. We laughed again. That was something that we enjoyed doing.

He pulled out my chair and signaled for me to sit. I sat. He walked around and took his seat. The conversation was boring. Yet, I pretended to be interested in his nonsensical rhetoric, even throwing in the occasional chuckle. That's not just the way it was on that day. That's how it always was. My new guy wasn't deep like KEN. He wasn't funny or witty like Antonio. He was quite dry. So, what was the appeal? He offered something that was different from all of the other men before him. He was my new KEN.

The Keepake Box Series is near and dear to my heart. Though all of the details are fictional, this is the story of millions of women worldwide. It is my deepest desire to shine a light on situations that have been downplayed, ignored, and suppressed.

While physical abuse is the most obvious, abuse comes in many forms. Understand that abuse can also be sexual, verbal, mental, emotional, even financial. None of those are healthy, and love doesn't hurt. Never be too ashamed to reach out, and never love anyone else to the point that you forget to love yourself.

*--Chandora*

Ps, be on the lookout for book 3!! Coming soon!!!!

www.ingramcontent.com/pod-product-compliance
Lightning Source LLC
Chambersburg PA
CBHW051832170626
46807CB00003B/1145

# SHERLOCK HOLMES
## MYSTERY MAGAZINE

VOL. 5, NO. 5                                      Issue #15

**Publisher: John Betancourt**
**Editor: Marvin Kaye**
**Non-fiction Editor: Carla Coupe**
**Assistant Editor: Steve Coupe**

*Sherlock Holmes Mystery Magazine* is published by Wildside Press, LLC. Single copies: $10.00 + $3.00 postage. U.S. subscriptions: $59.95 (postage paid) for the next 6 issues in the U.S.A., from: Wildside Press LLC, Subscription Dept. 9710 Traville Gateway Dr., #234; Rockville MD 20850. International subscriptions: see our web site at www.wildsidemagazines.com. Available as an ebook through all major ebook etailers, or our web site, www.wildsidemagazines.com.